WANTED: THE PERFECT HUSBAND

MARGERY SCOTT

MAIL-ORDER BRIDES OF SAPPHIRE SPRINGS

Miranda
Audra
Kathryn
Elise

OTHER HISTORICAL ROMANCES

Emma's Wish
Wild Wyoming Wind
Rose: Bride of Colorado
Mail-Order Melanie

MEDICAL ROMANCES

The Surgeon's Homecoming
Stranded with the Surgeon
The Firefighter and the Lady Doc

CONTEMPORARY ROMANCES

Winterlude

CHAPTER 1

*I*t was time.

Sybil Franklin opened the bedroom door and stepped inside for the first time since her mother's death.

She closed the door behind her and leaned her back against it, letting the memories wash over her. She breathed in the familiar lavender scent, feeling her mother's presence in the room she'd never left for more than four years before she died.

A layer of dust covered the surface of the fluted walnut dresser on the wall near the window and the night tables flanking the heavy four-poster bed that dominated the space.

Sybil's footsteps were muffled as she trudged across the carpet and gathered up the hand-knitted pink lap blanket from the rocking chair in the corner. She held it close to her chest as tears stung her eyes and rolled unheeded down her cheeks.

She glanced at the small clock on her mother's dressing table. It had stopped weeks ago, but she didn't need to see the time to know it was late afternoon.

Raindrops pattered against the window looking out onto the street, but life didn't stop, even for bad weather. Outside, carriages rolled by. People talked to each other as they passed the window. A dog barked.

Sybil's tears dripped onto the blanket clutched in her hands, but she let them fall until she was spent. Then, taking a few shuddery breaths, she folded it and placed it on the bed.

She'd had to give herself a stern talking-to to get her to the point of dealing with her mother's belongings, and unpleasant as she knew it would be, it had to be done eventually, and putting it off wouldn't make the job any easier.

For the next hour, she carefully folded and piled the dresses and winter coat still hanging in the wardrobe, and the blouses and shawls in the dresser drawers. Tomorrow, she'd take the clothes and her mother's shoes and boots to the church to donate to those less fortunate than herself.

She'd already kept a few personal items for herself —a music box that held the few pieces of jewelry her mother had owned, a magnifying glass her mother had used to read her precious books, a mother-of-pearl letter opener.

Finally, all that was left was a small trunk in the bottom of the wardrobe in the corner of the bedroom.

Crouching down, she wrapped her fingers around the iron handle on the side of the trunk and dragged it out of the wardrobe.

The trunk had been beautiful once, but now, the wood was weathered, the two leather straps wrapped around it cracked and dry. The lock was rusty, and the brass studs that decorated the lid were now almost obscured by a layer of dust as if it hadn't been opened in months.

Sybil had never seen the inside of the trunk. She'd asked her mother about it a few times over the years, and each time, she'd been told the contents were private and none of her business. Her mother had kept the trunk locked, and Sybil had never known where the key was hidden.

A memory suddenly surfaced in her brain. Once, when she was a girl and her mother had been outside working in the small vegetable garden behind the house, she'd taken a kitchen knife and gone into her mother's bedroom. She'd opened the wardrobe, climbed inside and pulled the door shut, intending to pry the lock open. She hadn't been there long when the door suddenly opened, bright light spilling in. She'd looked up to see her mother, hands planted on her hips, her eyes narrowed, her lips pressed together in anger. Sybil had learned very quickly—and harshly—that she was never to touch the trunk again.

What secrets did her mother have that she was so afraid of being discovered?

Even now, a feeling of guilt swelled inside Sybil as she held the brass key in her hand and prepared to open the trunk. She'd found the key hidden in the pages of a copy of *Pride and Prejudice* in her mother's dressing table. It had fallen out when she'd picked up the book, intending to put it back on the shelf in the parlor.

Her heart raced, and a chill washed over her. She sensed her mother looking down from above, a stern expression of disapproval on her face. With trembling fingers, she unbuckled the leather straps, then inserted the key into the brass lock and turned it. A moment later, she heard a slight click and the hasp sprang open.

Taking in a steadying breath, she lifted the lid. Stale air met her nose as she looked inside.

A dried flower. A yellowed ticket stub from a theater performance. A plain gold wedding band engraved with the words "forever mine".

But it was the stack of yellowed envelopes tied with a blue ribbon that drew Sybil's attention. Perhaps letters from her father to her mother before they married?

Sybil had never known her father. He'd perished in a fire when she was a baby.

She picked up the letters, taking note of the return address—Rocky Ridge, Colorado. Her brow furrowed. Surely if her father had spent time in Colorado, her mother would have mentioned it at one time or another.

Her curiosity piqued, Sybil untied the ribbon,

intending to read only the letter on top of the pile. Somehow, the letters slipped out of her grasp and slid to the polished hardwood floor. It was then the beginning of her name on one of the envelopes caught her eye. Her heart thudded behind her ribs as she plucked it out from beneath the others. The letter was addressed to her, and came from an attorney in Rocky Ridge.

The envelope had been opened, yet she'd never seen it before. Why had her mother hidden it from her?

With trembling fingers, she opened the flap and took out a single piece of paper.

Dear Miss Franklin,

It is with deep regret that I must notify you of the death of your father, Mr. Harvey Franklin.

As Mr. Franklin's attorney at the time of his death, it is my duty to inform you that you are the beneficiary of his entire estate. However, the will does specify that you must present yourself to my office within one year of the date of this letter to claim the said estate. Failure to do so will result in forfeiture of all claims against the estate.

Please contact me as soon as possible to make arrangements.

Yours sincerely,
B.A. Morgan,
Attorney-at-Law

The letter in her hand was dated almost ten months before.

Sybil's heartbeat stuttered. The room swam, and she slumped to the floor, her back flat against the wall. She couldn't wrap her mind around the fact that her mother had lied to her. Her whole life, she'd believed her father had died when she was an infant, when in reality, he'd been alive and well until less than a year ago.

Her mind in a whirl, the letter slipped from her fingers and fluttered to the floor. Her gaze shifted to the rest of the pile. She flipped through the other letters absently, her mind not really registering what she was seeing. There were at least twenty letters in the pile, all addressed to her mother in the same handwriting, the postmarks dated every few months from the time she was less than a year old until his last letter a month before his death.

"Sybil? What on earth are you doing? What are those?"

The feminine voice shattered the haze in Sybil's brain. Startled, she looked up.

Her best friend, Violet Palmer, stood in the doorway. "I knocked but you didn't answer. I was worried … whatever is the matter?"

Shadows filled the room, and although it seemed as if it had only been seconds, Sybil realized she'd been sitting on the floor for quite some time. "I …"

Scooping up the letters and stacking them into a pile, she quickly placed them back in the trunk. She was anxious to read the letters, but she'd prefer to read them in private.

She handed the letter from the attorney to Violet, then slowly got to her feet.

Violet's eyes widened as she scanned the paper. "Where did you get this?" she asked in a disbelieving tone when she'd finished reading. "I mean … is it possible …?"

"I don't know," Sybil said, retrieving the letter from Violet and slipping it back into the envelope. She slid the envelope into the pocket of the pale yellow apron she was wearing over her dark brown day dress. "It seems very official, but …"

Questions tumbled through her brain at such a rate she couldn't form a proper sentence. "How could … Did my mother …What …?"

Violet rested her hand on Sybil's arm. "Come downstairs. I'll make tea and we'll talk about this."

A half hour later, Sybil was no closer to understanding why her mother had lied about her father. He hadn't died. He'd left them, and yet, he'd kept in touch. She'd known two other men who'd left wives and children behind and gone west, but as far as she knew, the families had never heard from either of the men again.

If her father hadn't wanted them, why had he kept writing to them all these years? If her mother loved him, why didn't she go with him? Or, if she no longer loved him, why did she keep his letters? And why had she hidden the last letter, the letter addressed to Sybil, in the middle of the pile? Since it was the last letter, wouldn't it have made more sense that it would be on top?

Questions swirled in her mind, questions she hoped she'd find answers to in the letters she'd left upstairs.

She did have an answer to one burning question she'd had for years, though. Whenever the postman had brought letters for her mother, he'd never given them to Sybil, but had always been invited upstairs to give them to her mother personally. Sybil had never understood why her mother was so insistent upon it, considering it was highly improper to entertain a man in a lady's private quarters. Now she understood why. Her mother hadn't wanted Sybil to see the letters from her father.

Anger smoldered inside her—anger at her mother and even at the postman who'd kept her mother's secret. The postman had had no reason to feel any loyalty toward her. But her mother … she felt betrayed by the one person she'd trusted most.

"I wonder what the inheritance is," Violet commented, setting the china teapot on the table in the dining room, dragging Sybil's thoughts back to the matter at hand.

Sybil shook her head. "I have no idea."

"You have to go to Colorado immediately and claim the inheritance. You don't have any time to waste."

"I don't know … I mean, I didn't even know he existed. What could he possibly have left me? And to travel all that way … alone … Colorado isn't even a state, and it's practically at the other end of the country."

Violet poured the tea into two matching cups and set one in front of Sybil. "How many times have you told me over the past few years how much you wanted to see the world?"

"I loved my mother. I never resented—"

Violet rested her hand on Sybil's arm. "I know that. But she's passed on. You have no ties here now. No responsibilities. I'll miss you terribly, but there's no reason to stay here."

Sybil dropped a sugar cube into her tea and began to stir as Violet's words rumbled around in her brain. What Violet said was true. There was nothing keeping her in Ohio now that her mother was gone. She'd spent the past four years of her life caring for her, giving up any chance of marriage and children of her own. She had no life at all to speak of outside these walls.

And now … to discover the secret her mother had kept from her …

"Have you ever even been out of Ohio?" Violet asked.

Sybil shook her head. "I haven't been any farther than Columbus."

"There's a whole wide world out there, and now that you're free—"

Free. Yes, she was free, as Violet put it. No husband, no children, no other family. Nothing other than her own fear of taking a chance and possibly changing her life for the better. "I'll think about it."

"You don't have time to think about it," Violet reminded her. "According to the date on the letter and the stipulation you have to get there within a year, you only have until the end of July, and it's already June. You need to go now or not at all."

Sybil took a sip of tea, the steaming liquid warming the chill that had settled inside her. She had to think. Hadn't she always been taught to weigh every fact before she made a decision?

Yet Violet was right. She didn't have the luxury of time. She had to decide. Soon.

"I'll go to Colorado," she said, surprised to hear the words leaving her mouth. "For some reason I don't understand, my mother didn't give me the chance to know my father for myself, but at least I might be able to get to know him through his friends and neighbors."

"I think that's a splendid idea," Violet gushed.

Another idea sprang into Sybil's mind. She leaned across the table, grabbed Violet's hand and peered at her. "Come with me."

"Violet's dark blue eyes widened. "Me? Why—"

"Yes. It's not proper for a woman to travel alone, and the journey would be so much more pleasant with company."

"I can't. I have a job."

Sybil's brows arched. "You aren't going to tell me you enjoy working at the factory, are you?"

"No," Violet said with a bitter laugh. "And Mr. Pettigrew is becoming increasingly … demanding. It's quite uncomfortable."

"Then come with me."

"I would love to, but I can't right now. Papa needs me."

Sybil sighed.

"Once he marries the widow Brown," Violet said, "I'll be a burden to both of them. I'm sure they'd be quite happy if I wasn't underfoot, and to be honest, I'd rather not be privy to the intimate details of their newly married status. I do have some savings …" A slow smile lifted her lips and a spark of excitement filled her eyes. "So, if you decide to stay in Colorado, as soon as Papa is married, I'll come."

"Wonderful." Sybil got up and began to pace the length of the room, her mind swirling with the preparations she'd have to make for the trip she was sure would change her life.

CHAPTER 2

A slate-grey sky filled with the promise of rain greeted Sybil when she climbed out of the stagecoach in front of the Wells Fargo office in Rocky Ridge six weeks later.

"This is certainly not what I expected," Sybil said to the driver, keeping her voice low enough that the people waiting on the boardwalk wouldn't be able to hear her. "The town is almost exactly like what I left at home."

Brooksbank, the town where she'd grown up in Ohio, was small, primitive by some standards. Somehow, this town so many miles from home felt comfortable, familiar. While the buildings back in Ohio were mostly brick and these were constructed of wood with false fronts and boardwalks to avoid having to deal with mud and dirt when going from one building to another, the main street seemed very much like the streets back home.

But instead of farmland as far as the eye could see in Ohio, here, in the distance, jagged mountains of varying shades of green and gold and purple reached into the sunless sky.

The street was busy and crowded with wagons and people. Two men she assumed were miners were leading mules down the middle of the street, and several ladies stood together, chatting in front of a dressmaker's shop.

"Here's your bags, miss," he said, ignoring her comment. "You got somebody meeting you?"

"No," she replied.

"Got a place to stay?"

She nodded. "I arranged for a room at a boarding house run by a Mrs. Virginia Morgan."

The driver nodded. "It's just around the corner that way," he said, pointing. He looked down at the trunk and carpetbag at her feet. "You want me to take these into the office then until you find somebody to take them to the boarding house for you?"

She smiled at him. "I would appreciate that. Do you know where I might find Mr. Morgan, the attorney?"

"Sure do," he said. "His office is a little bit past the saloon. You can't miss it."

While the driver disappeared inside the Wells Fargo office with her bags, Sybil hurried in the direction the stagecoach driver had indicated. On the way, she passed several other businesses that would never be located on a main street back in Brooksbank—the undertaker, a mining assay office, even the jailhouse. Her cheeks flamed in embarrassment when she passed by a saloon on the other side of the street where four soiled doves were lounging on the second-floor balcony and waving to the cowboys passing by.

Just as the driver had promised, she caught sight of the sign outside a small building with a large glass window. She opened the door and went inside, pausing just inside the entrance. "Mr. Morgan?" she asked the man standing at a pot-bellied stove near the back wall. He was holding a metal coffeepot in his hand.

He turned to face her. "I am," he responded, putting the mug down and crossing the office. "But you can call me Brett. We tend not to stand on formality much here."

He gestured toward a chair in front of a desk near the window. "Please come in and sit down."

Sybil did as he suggested, perching on the edge of a chair directly across from him.

"Can I get you a cup of coffee?" he asked. "I was just about to pour myself one."

"No, thank you, but you go ahead."

He finished pouring his coffee, then crossed to his desk and sat down, setting the mug on a small round piece of cork. "Now, how can I help you?"

Sybil dug the letter out of her reticule and handed it to him. "My name is Sybil Franklin," she began. "This letter came from you regarding my father, Harvey Franklin."

She sat quietly and waited as the lawyer's eyes

scanned the paper. Then he put the letter down and looked up at her, studying her for a few moments. "You're Harvey's daughter?"

She nodded, pulling another envelope out of her reticule. "I do have a letter of introduction from the pastor of my church in Ohio—"

"That's fine, although I wouldn't be concerned if you didn't have anything to prove your identity," he said. "You're the spitting image of Harvey."

Her heart squeezed tight at that piece of information.

"My condolences on your loss," the lawyer continued.

"Thank you."

"It's a shame he didn't get a chance to see you before he passed," Brett said. "You barely made the deadline."

It bothered Sybil that it appeared she hadn't been interested in knowing her father while he was alive, and that she'd waited until the last minute to come to Colorado. She didn't have to explain her late arrival, but for some reason, it was important to her that he knew it wasn't her fault.

For the next several minutes, she explained the circumstances surrounding her discovery of the letters her mother had hidden from her and how she'd found out her father hadn't died when she was a baby as she'd been led to believe.

When she was finished, the lawyer leaned back in his chair. "Well, I can tell you Harvey had no idea that you didn't know about him. He was under the impression you didn't want to have any contact with him."

"I came as soon as I found out. I only wish …" She left the words unsaid. Wishing never made anything come true. "I don't understand why my mother lied to me," she added. "And now that she's gone, I'll likely never know."

"That is unfortunate," he said in agreement. "I can't tell you much, only that I understand he came here back in the late forties, long before I got here. He was a well-liked and well-respected member of the community."

A bittersweet smile quirked her lips. At least he hadn't been a scoundrel or a criminal, she thought.

"Can you tell me what happened?" she asked. "How did he die? Was he ill?"

Brett shook his head. "Your father was healthy as a horse. Never had a sick day in all the time I knew him. He was out riding in the foothills by himself. His horse threw him for some reason and he broke his neck. Nobody knew until his horse showed up the next day."

Sybil's heart lurched. How long did he lie on the ground, injured, alone, before he died?

As if the lawyer could read her thoughts, he continued. "According to the doc, he died instantly."

"I'm glad to hear he didn't suffer."

"He didn't." Brett stacked a pile of papers on his desk and set them aside. "Now I'm sure you're anxious to know the details of your father's will."

She *was* anxious, not to find out what he'd left her,

but she couldn't help hoping that his will might hold a clue as to why he'd left them so many years ago and why he'd kept writing to her mother.

Brett got up and crossed to the floor-to-ceiling shelves lining the far wall of his office. He reached up and took down a metal box from the top shelf.

After he sat back down, he took off the lid and withdrew several sheets of paper and a small canvas bag.

Sybil's heart raced, but whether it was from anticipation or hesitation, she couldn't say.

Brett scanned the legal-looking papers and stacked them in front of him. "Your father lived here for more than twenty years," he said, "but he never married and had no other family."

That piece of information surprised her. Why had he never remarried?"

"Did he never divorce my mother?" she asked.

Brett shook his head. "Not that I know of. If he did, I didn't handle it. And since I took care of all his other legal matters, I'd assume I would have dealt with a divorce too if there had been one."

If they'd never divorced, did that mean he'd still loved her mother. Or had he remained married for some other reason?

"You are the sole beneficiary of his entire estate," Brett continued.

Sybil was confused. "I don't understand. If my parents weren't divorced, wasn't my mother his next of kin? Why didn't his estate go to her?"

"I can't answer that," he replied. "Your father specified his estate should go to you and you alone."

She was sure he'd had his reasons for what he did, but what they were, she'd never know. Her heart sank and she couldn't help feeling disappointed that she now had more questions than answers.

"You'll be a wealthy young woman soon," Brett said, handing her a document that she saw was deed to a piece of land. "This is the deed to the Franklin Ranch and all the buildings on the property.

"A ranch? He left me a ranch?"

"That's right," he replied. "A sizable piece of property along with a five-bedroom house and several barns and outbuildings."

"A ranch." The words came out on a whoosh of air. Why would he leave her a ranch when he was well aware she'd grown up in a town and knew nothing about ranching? Still, her curiosity got the better of her. "What kind of ranch?"

"Cattle mostly. Your father ran one of the best cattle operations around. He was a born rancher. But it's been sorely neglected since nobody's occupied it in almost a year."

She was finding it hard to understand how a herd of cattle could survive when no one was caring for it. "So the cattle are gone now?"

"No," Brett said. "The ranch foreman decided not to stay on after your father died, and left a few days later. One of your father's neighbors, Joel Hutchings, has been looking after the cattle. Of course, the cost of feed, etc. as well as a small stipend has been deducted from the estate account."

"Of course."

"There's still enough money left to repair the house and the property and give you time to get the ranch back into working order. However, once you fulfill the terms of the will, you're welcome to sell it. I've already had an offer to buy the entire ranch and contents."

The figure he mentioned made her gasp. It was more money than she could imagine. Something he'd said earlier suddenly popped into her brain. "You said I'd be a wealthy woman *soon*. What did you mean?"

"There are some conditions in the will that have to be met."

She remembered him mentioning terms as well, but her brain hadn't registered it. It sounded ominous. "What kind of conditions?"

"The will stipulates you forfeit any claim on the ranch if you aren't married within one year of the date of his death."

"One year? Why … why, that's only …" She paused, calculating how much time she'd have to find a husband.

"Exactly thirteen days."

"That's ridiculous. I can't get married in less than two weeks." Not only did she have no intention of marrying anyone, she couldn't even if she wanted to. Since she'd reached marrying age, she'd spent every minute of her day caring for her mother. She'd never even had a suitor.

"I'm sure your father expected you to come to Rocky Ridge before the time limit was almost up. But that's not all. There is one other condition."

Her heart sank. "What?"

"You and your husband have to live on the ranch until the third anniversary of your father's death."

Two years? It wasn't enough that to gain her inheritance she'd be forced to marry a stranger, but she'd have to live with him, share her home—and likely her bed—with him for the next two years or so. The whole idea was preposterous.

"What happens to the ranch if I don't meet these conditions?"

"The ranch will go to a Mr. Armitage in Wyoming."

Armitage? The name was familiar. She'd heard her mother mention her father's cousin in Wyoming, the man who'd tried to prevent their marriage, and had even gone as far as to try to bribe her father into breaking off their engagement.

"Wait a minute. Let me get this straight. I have to marry within the next two weeks or so and live on the ranch with him until the third anniversary of my father's death otherwise it goes to someone in Wyoming."

"I'm afraid so."

"Did you know my father well?"

"Fairly well, I suppose."

"Then tell me, why would my father do that to me?

Why would he bring me all this way only to force me to marry to gain an inheritance?"

"That I don't have an answer for, Miss Franklin."

She needed to walk. She needed a clear head to be able to make sense of the situation she suddenly found herself in. Walking always helped her to solve a problem, to make decisions and to put things into perspective.

She got up. "Thank you for your time, Mr. Morgan. You've given me a lot to think about. I do need some time to consider my options. I'll be in touch as soon as I've made a decision." Then she turned and walked out of the office onto the boardwalk.

For the next half hour, Sybil walked the entire length of Rocky Ridge's main street. When she reached the end, she climbed a hill to a small cemetery, hoping to find her father's resting place there. There was no stone marking his grave, so she turned and retraced her steps back to Mr. Morgan's office.

By the time she reached his office, she'd made her decision.

The attorney looked up and smiled as she entered and crossed to his desk. "Mr. Morgan," she began, "where exactly is the Franklin Ranch?"

"It's about four miles east ... past the oak that got hit by lightning a few months ago ... you're going to have trouble finding it. If you don't mind waiting a few minutes, I'd be happy to take you so you can see it."

"I'd appreciate that."

"Are you thinking about staying and working the ranch?" he asked, packing the documents back into the metal box.

"I'm not thinking about it," she replied. "I've already decided. I'm staying."

*D*evin McGregor stopped sweeping the boardwalk in front of the mercantile and leaned on the broom handle as Curly Ames tossed the two lengths of heavy rope into the wagon bed as if they were no heavier than balls of string.

"That's a lot of rope," Devin commented. "Something special going on out at the Triple M?"

"More horses to break is all," Curly said. "We could use an extra hand, too. You sure you don't want a job?"

Devin shook his head. "I'm happy here."

It was a lie, and he and Curly both knew it. He should be out on the range, mending fences, putting up hay for the winter and moving cattle, not sweeping floors and stacking cans on shelves. Not to mention dealing with women complaining that the mercantile didn't carry the exact color of fabric they wanted or that the price of coffee was too high. It wasn't as if he had any say in what stock Elias Todd carried or set the prices, but he took the brunt of their anger.

"If you change your mind …" Curly let the sentence die out as he climbed into the wagon and picked up the reins.

"I know." Devin did know. There was a job waiting for him at the Triple M. Fresh air, hard physical work that would strain a man's muscles and make him sweat. Work he loved.

But he was done with ranching. He'd sunk everything he had into the small spread he'd bought four years before. And he'd lost it all six months ago.

"Devin!"

The voice calling his name made him cringe. Not that he didn't like Elias Todd as a friend. He did. But working for the man—that was a whole different story.

Since he'd been working for Elias in the mercantile for the past few weeks, he'd developed a real admiration for Cammie, Elias's daughter. She'd been spending her free time behind that counter since she was little more than a girl. It was no wonder she couldn't wait to leave Rocky Ridge. He would have likely run away from home years ago.

With a sigh, Devin set the broom against the wall and went back inside. "What do you need, Elias?"

Elias was braced against the counter, a crutch under one arm. "I have your pay," he said, handing Devin a few bills from the pile in his hand. "Here you are," he said. "I'll need you for another month or so, but I think that's all. I should be healed up enough by then to get the work done myself." Then he turned and wobbled his way to the end of the counter and then disappeared through the curtain separating the front of the store from the storeroom.

Devin didn't bother to count the bills. He trusted Elias, and he knew exactly how much he'd been paid—enough to survive on, but not much more.

He should be thankful he had a job, though. He knew that. Since he'd lost the ranch, he'd had trouble finding steady work. A day here, a week there until Elias had fallen down a set of stairs and broken his ankle. He was on the mend, but still wasn't capable of doing any of the heavy lifting, so he'd hired Devin to help out while he recovered.

The future weighed heavily on Devin's mind. Once Elias was back on his feet, he'd be out of work again.

He missed the outdoors and the scent of pine and cedar filling his nose. He missed the freedom of riding the range. But most of all, he missed having something he could call his own.

Curly didn't understand why he wouldn't work for Cade Morgan at the Triple M since Devin and Cade had been friends for years. Devin didn't understand it either, only that he knew he couldn't stand working the land for somebody else—even Cade—when he'd lost his own.

He'd heard from some of the cowboys who'd been in the store the day before that the Grainger spread would be coming up for sale in the next few weeks when Mac Grainger left to go and live with his daughter in New Mexico.

Devin knew the parcel they were talking about. It was level, near the river, and had a log house on a hill overlooking the river that was perfect for a small family. And the price was right.

He looked down at the bills in his hand and let out a short laugh. Even if he wanted to start up again—which he didn't—by the time he could afford to buy another piece of land, he'd likely be too old to work it.

The bell above the door jingled as the door opened and Mrs. Lundstrom marched in, the feathers covering her bonnet fluttering in the breeze she created. "Good afternoon, Mr. McGregor."

"Afternoon, Miz Lundstrom," he replied, pasting a smile on his face. "What can I do for you today?"

It took her almost a half hour to decide on a color, but between gossip and complaints, she finally left with one spool of thread and a jar of preserves.

When the door finally closed behind her, Devin let out a sigh. How was he going to survive this another month?

Sybil was quiet on the ride back from the Franklin Ranch. Mr. Morgan had been right. She never would have found the property herself.

And as he'd promised, he'd driven her past fields of wildflowers and high grasses to her father's ranch. She hadn't bothered examining the fields since she had no idea what she'd be looking for, but her heart had sunk when he'd stopped the buggy in front of the house. It was in a sad state of repair. Broken windows, paint beginning to peel, a front porch that sagged when she stepped on it.

Yet the construction of the house seemed solid enough, and with some elbow grease, she was sure it could be brought back to its former glory.

Something about the ranch drew her in. Perhaps it was the open land, overgrown though it was. Perhaps it was the mountains—the same mountains that had captured her the minute she'd stepped off the stage— rising to disappear in the fog that blanketed their peaks now. She'd never seen a sight more spectacular.

Or perhaps it was something else, something mystical she couldn't explain. Somehow, she'd sensed her father's presence welcoming her and making her feel as if she belonged there, which was all the more strange since she'd never met him.

"Well, Miss Franklin, what do you think?" Mr. Morgan asked as they started back on the trail toward town. "Still thinking about settling here?"

"It is pretty rundown," she said. "but … I want it." She was surprised to hear the words coming out of her mouth, but it was true. She wanted the Franklin Ranch. She'd never wanted anything more in her life.

"You do? When you said earlier that you'd decided to stay, you hadn't seen the condition the ranch is in. I was almost positive you'd change your mind once you came out here and saw the place for yourself."

"I haven't changed my mind," she said. "I'm staying." There was no logical explanation for the sudden desire … no, it was need … to be part of her father's world. She'd never even known the man, and now, she was about to marry a stranger so she could carry on what he'd started.

It was a legacy from a man who'd obviously still cared about her even after so many years, a legacy she couldn't bring herself to give up without a fight.

Could the trip to Colorado have addled her brain? She'd heard the air was thinner here because of the altitude. Perhaps that was what was wrong—there wasn't enough air getting to her brain.

Even so, she couldn't stop herself from shifting in her seat to face the lawyer. "So, the next order of business is to find myself a husband. Thirteen days, right?"

"That's right."

"Do you know of anyone who might be willing to marry me?"

He glanced over at her and smiled. "Miss Franklin, if it's not too improper of me to say since I'm a married man, I don't think you'll have any trouble finding a man who'd be happy to marry you."

"He has to be the perfect man," she pointed out. "A man who's kind and generous and a hard worker and who'll be a good husband and father to any children we might have. Do you have anyone you could recommend?"

He kept his gaze on the trail ahead for a short time, then smiled. "As a matter of fact, I do," he said. "When we get back to town, I'll write his name down and show you where you can find him."

"Excellent. And if you wouldn't mind taking me to the boarding house, they're expecting me. I'll go and meet my perfect husband in the morning."

Sybil tidied her hair and changed her dress, then descended the stairs to the dining room in the boarding house later that afternoon.

Virginia Morgan, the owner, was putting a steaming bowl of stew on the table as she entered. "Ah, there you are," she said with a smile. "I thought you might be resting and didn't want to bother you."

Sybil returned her smile. "I wasn't, but I'm sure if I was, the wonderful aroma would have woken me."

Virginia took her place opposite her husband. "Come and sit down, and meet the other guests and we'll get to know each other better."

Sybil had already met Virginia's husband, Will and their son, Jeremy.

"This is Amos Langley," Virginia said, smiling at the burly man seated beside her at the table.

Sybil moved to hold out her hand, then decided against it. Dirt was ingrained in his fingernails and his hands. She gave him a faint smile, only to be polite. "Nice to meet you."

Amos wiped his mouth on a napkin but missed the food clinging to his bushy grey beard. "Howdy, ma'am," he said, a moment before he broke off a chunk of bread and rammed it into his mouth.

"And Jeb Carpenter," Virginia said.

The gaunt man with a shock of mud-brown hair sitting beside Amos nodded in her direction, but didn't speak.

"Miz Morgan told us your problem," Amos said, not bothering to swallow his bread before he spoke. "I'd be honored to marry you. I've been wanting a family for a long time now."

Mercy! The thought of spending even one night with the man made her shudder inwardly.

Jeb put his fork down and peered at her. "If you don't want Amos," he said, "I'll marry you."

The man looked like a strong wind would blow him over. She couldn't trust that he'd be able to handle the heavy labor ranching entailed.

"I appreciate the offer, gentlemen," she began, choosing her words carefully, "but I'd like to take some time to really consider my options."

"Sure thing, darlin'," Amos said, digging into his stew again. "But when you're ready, you just let me know when and where and I'll be there."

Sybil plastered a smile on her face that she didn't feel. "Of course."

The rest of the meal passed in relative comfort, and Sybil retired to her room soon after. As she dressed for bed and braided her dark brown hair in front of the mirror, the reality of her situation hit her. Worry mixed with sadness, draining her energy until it was almost too much effort to crawl into bed.

She had to find a husband in less than two weeks, and if men like Amos Langley and Jeb Carpenter were her only options, she'd have no choice but to give up the ranch that had suddenly become more important to her than anything else in her life.

Sybil paid special attention to her appearance the next morning. After all, she was hoping to meet her future husband within a few hours and she wanted to make a good impression.

She took extra time to pin her hair into a loose knot at the nape of her neck, leaving a few curls to frame her face. Then she slipped into a dark blue dress that she knew complimented her fair skin.

"You look lovely this morning," Virginia commented when she went downstairs for breakfast.

"Thank you," she replied, surprised—and yes, pleased—to find only Jeremy and Virginia at the table. Platters of eggs, bacon and sausage were laid out on a sideboard against the wall. Slices of fresh bread and a pot of coffee sat beside mugs, plates and silverware.

"Can I go now, Ma?" Jeremy piped up as Sybil poured a cup of coffee and took her place at the table. "I finished my eggs."

Virginia turned to her son. "You may if you can," she told him with a smile, "and you can and may put your dishes on the counter before you go."

"I hope you aren't upset with me," Virginia said to Sybil after Jeremy left. "I was telling Will why you'd come to town and Amos happened to come into the kitchen in the middle. I wouldn't have mentioned it to them otherwise."

Sybil gave her a soft smile. "Not at all. I'm sure it'll be all over town soon anyway." She filled a plate and set it on the table, then slid into a chair.

"I didn't expect either Amos or Will to offer for your hand, though. You don't want either one of them," Virginia told her.

Sybil chuckled. "They aren't exactly what I had in mind. I'm hoping Mr. McGregor will be the one."

"You could do a lot worse than Devin McGregor," Virginia said. "He's a fine-looking man, almost as handsome as my Will. I wouldn't get my hopes up if I were you, though. There are a lot of females in this town who'd be happy to marry him, but he hasn't shown interest in any of them."

"Oh." This piece of information was a little disheartening. If none of the women in town had managed to get him to the altar, what were the chances she could? And in less than two weeks?

"Not since he lost his ranch a few months back," Virginia went on as she dropped a lump of sugar into her coffee. "Seems like he lost interest in everything after that."

The fact that Devin McGregor had lost his ranch was important. If he wasn't capable of holding onto his own ranch, why would Brett Morgan assume he could run hers? "What happened that he lost it?"

"That's for him to tell you," Virginia said, "but if I were you, it wouldn't stop me marrying him. And the sooner you get over to the mercantile and meet him, the sooner you might find out."

CHAPTER 4

Sybil walked down the boardwalk, her steps slowing the closer she got to the mercantile. With every step, the sound of activity around her faded away under the erratic rhythm of her pulse drumming in her ears. She'd lost her mind, she decided. How could she even consider asking a perfect stranger to marry her? Back east, they would have locked her up in an asylum for the rest of her life, she was sure.

But she had no other choice if she wanted to keep the ranch. She'd lain awake most of the night trying to understand why she was so determined to keep it instead of relinquishing her claim and going back to Ohio. She wasn't a frivolous person so her mother's estate provided more than enough to support her as long as she wasn't careless with her finances. She didn't need her father's money.

She'd been no closer to an answer by the time the

scarlet rays of dawn filtered through the curtains at the window and she'd heard the sounds of the town awakening outside.

All she'd known was that she'd do what she had to do to keep the ranch.

Now, here she was, about to propose marriage to a man she'd never seen before.

Her stomach was so twisted in knots she feared she might embarrass herself, but she took in several deep calming breaths and opened the mercantile door. A bell above the door jangled as she went inside, her body trembling. The aromas of coffee and spices blending with tobacco and coal oil filled her nose.

It took a moment for her eyes to adjust from the sunshine to the interior of the store, but as soon as it did, she noticed the man behind the counter. He looked up and met her gaze when she closed the door behind her.

Was this Devin McGregor? Virginia had mentioned how handsome he was, but her description hadn't done this man justice. Hair the color of wet wheat grazed the collar of his tan shirt. He had a strong chin and square jaw, and his broad shoulders and a muscled chest gave her confidence that he could handle hard work. His brownish-gold eyes ringed by dark lashes held a hint of sadness.

Yes, he was much more handsome than Virginia had led her to believe. Just looking at him did something to her insides, a strange sensation that fluttered through her veins. *Mercy!* She'd never felt anything like this before.

She was tempted to turn around and run, but both the lawyer and Virginia had recommended him. If she didn't at least ask, who knew what kind of man she might end up with?

Taking in one last breath, she began. "Mr. McGregor?"

Devin had never seen the woman addressing him before. He was sure he wouldn't have forgotten her. Chocolate-colored hair that glistened in the sunshine streaming through the window, wide brown eyes with perfectly arched brows, and full lips. Her dark blue dress hugged curves made to fit against a man's body. She was downright beautiful.

As she crossed toward him, his heartbeat seemed to ripple against his ribs. It was only when she got closer that he noticed the tension in the way she moved, so rigid she looked like she'd snap if she moved the wrong way. Her hands were gripping her reticule so tightly her knuckles were white.

She looked like she was scared spitless, but of what, he had no idea. Surely she wasn't scared of him. Or was she?

"That's me," Devin replied when she mentioned his name. He gave her the brightest smile he could conjure up to try to make her relax a little. "What can I do for you?"

She introduced herself.

So this was Harvey's daughter, the daughter he'd always figured he'd go back east and see again before he died.

"Pleased to make your acquaintance, ma'am," he said.

"Please, call me Sybil."

"Only if you call me Devin," he said. "Sorry for your loss. I know your Pa was hoping he'd see you again one day. Too bad you couldn't get here until now."

Was it her imagination that the tone of his voice held a note of criticism?

"Well …" she said, tamping down the twinge of irritation she felt. He obviously wasn't aware of the circumstances, so she couldn't really blame him. She might have the same impression without knowing the facts. "I'm not quite sure how to say this, but Mr. Morgan said—"

He held up a hand to stop her. "Hang on," he said. "Which Mr. Morgan?"

For a second or two, she didn't answer, so he explained. "There's a lot of them in these parts, so it would be handy to know which one you're talking about."

"Oh. Mr. Brett Morgan, the attorney."

Devin nodded. "Okay then, go on."

She didn't speak for a few more moments, as if she was trying to find the right words. "As I said, Mr.

Morgan suggested I come and see you, that perhaps you could help me with a problem I have."

"I'd be happy to help you if I can, but first you'll have to tell me what the problem is."

"Of course." She twisted the straps of her reticule until they were wound as tight as what he expected her nerves were. Then she looked up at him. "I have to … what I mean is, I need …"

"You need what?" he prodded.

She took a deep breath, letting it out slowly. "I need a husband."

Devin could have sworn the woman was asking him to marry her, but he must have heard wrong. Didn't he? "You want a husband?" he asked.

She looked away, as if she couldn't force herself to look him square in the eye.

"I don't *want* a husband. I *need* a husband," she repeated.

He let out a soft whistle. "That's what I thought you said, but I figured I was hearing things. And Brett Morgan thought I might be the one to ask?"

If the woman had mentioned Trey's name—or even Heath's - instead of Brett's, he would have been sure it was some kind of prank. But not Brett.

She nodded. "I realize this must come as a shock, but time is of the utmost importance. I just got here yesterday and I don't have time to be courted properly."

"You mind telling me why you're in such a hurry to

get married that you'd marry a man you don't even know?"

"Of course." She let out a short laugh. "I realize this is quite unusual," she began, then for the next few minutes explained everything that had happened. "So you see, Mr. McGregor, since you are unmarried and you're familiar with ranching, you're the obvious choice."

Devin couldn't believe what he was hearing, but he wasn't about to get married, especially to a woman he'd never seen before a few minutes ago.

Sure, he'd been a rancher, but he'd lost everything. And he wasn't going to take the chance again, especially when it was somebody else's ranch he could lose. "Look, ma'am, I'm sure you're a nice lady and you'll make some man a good wife one day, but not me."

She couldn't say she was surprised at his reaction. If the tables were turned, she'd probably have the same response. After all, he didn't know her at all and she was asking him to spend a lifetime with her—or two years, anyway.

"But it's only temporary—"

"I'm sure Brett thought that since I was a rancher once that I'd be the most likely person to help you out, and I'm flattered you'd want to marry me, but I don't have any intentions of getting married. Not for two years. Not even for two days."

"I see." Her cheeks flamed. "Then I apologize for wasting your time. Good day."

He watched as she spun around and, drawing herself up to her full height—which was barely up to his chin, he noticed, she marched out the door.

Sybil blinked back tears as she shuffled down the board-walk toward the boarding house a few minutes later.

She'd never felt so humiliated in her life. She hadn't really expected Devin McGregor to jump at the chance to marry her and become a ranch owner again, but she had thought he might at least consider it for a few minutes before he turned her down. She'd offered him a piece of land that, according to Brett Morgan, was quite valuable even though it didn't look it right now. She'd offered him a future. Yet apparently he found it prefer-able to work for someone else in a shop instead.

The question was, what was she going to do now? The minute she'd seen him behind the counter, she'd been drawn to him, and now, the prospect of marrying someone like Amos or Jeb seemed even worse than it had the day before.

Surely there were some good men in this town. All she had to do was find one. One who was willing and able to work hard for two years. In return, she would be a good wife. If, after the ranch was legally hers, she and her husband didn't want to continue with the marriage, she was sure they could come to some kind of mutual arrangement that would benefit them both.

Where does a woman look for a husband? she wondered. Back in Ohio, she'd heard of men in the west who advertised for wives in the newspapers.

But she was already in the west. Since there was a shortage of women here, there would be no point in men advertising for a bride in the local newspapers. So what was she going to do?

As she passed the sheriff's office, she noticed the wanted posters nailed to the wall outside the door for everyone to see. An idea tickled her brain.

It was too preposterous to even consider, wasn't it? It was definitely not an acceptable way for a young lady to find a husband. But what alternative did she have? And if it was perfectly acceptable for a man to advertise for a spouse, why shouldn't a woman have the freedom to do the same?

She couldn't nail her advertisement to the wall outside the sheriff's office, but when she thought about it, she remembered she had seen a few notices tacked to one of the walls in the mercantile when she was there earlier.

It might not work, but she had to try. Time was running out.

Her mind made up, she hurried back to the boarding house. A short time later, she read the advertisement she'd drawn up on a piece of paper she'd gotten from Virginia.

Her hopes grew as she hurried back toward the

mercantile. Surely there were unmarried men in town who qualified. She didn't need Devin McGregor!

Devin was surprised when the door opened and Sybil walked in. She hadn't been gone more than an hour or two, and he couldn't think of any reason why she'd be back.

She wasn't smiling, but even with a frown creasing her forehead and her lips pressed into a thin line, she was still one of the prettiest women he'd ever laid eyes on.

Setting the feather duster down on the stool behind him, he rested his hands on the counter. "What can I do for you, Sybil?"

She eyed him squarely, her dark brown eyes sparkling.

"I'd like to put this notice up," she said, lifting the advertisement she'd designed to eye level.

"You would?"

"That's right. I noticed earlier that there were several notices on the wall. I'd like to add mine."

"Okay," he said. "What are you advertising for?"

"A husband."

"What?" He reached for the piece of paper in her hand, his fingers grazing hers.

Something in the touch of her skin warmed him, and

he quickly plucked the notice from her hand so he could escape the unwelcome sensation.

Her eyes widened, but whether it was because she'd felt the same burst of heat, he couldn't say.

He scanned the firm handwriting on the paper in his hand. It looked just like a wanted poster, except the heading read: "Wanted: The Perfect Husband. Underneath it listed only four qualities she was looking for—age 25-35, hard worker, of sound mind and body, and ranching experience.

She really expected him to post a notice like that in the back of the store? "That's crazy. You can't do that."

"Why not?"

"Because … because you don't advertise for a husband, that's why not." When she'd proposed to him earlier, she'd said she didn't have time for a normal courtship, so he did have to give her credit for coming up with a way to attract a man. But it was the kind of man she'd be attracting he was worried about.

"You turned me down, and I don't have any other prospects. I can't think of another way to find a husband in such a short time. You came highly recommended, but you refused. What else can I do?"

He had no answer. He only knew she was asking for trouble. "This is not a good idea."

"Why not?"

"Because there are a lot of men in this town who'll take advantage of your situation." He didn't want to point out that there were also a lot of men in Rocky

Ridge who'd take advantage of her. She was small, delicate-looking, and wouldn't be able to put up much of a fight against some of the cowboys who rode into town on a Saturday night from the nearby ranches.

"I'll have to take that chance," she said.

"You're going to get a lot of offers," he went on, "but I'll bet you wouldn't want to spend even an hour with most of them."

"That's for me to decide."

"Why don't you let me find out about the men you're going to see first?" Why he'd offered, he couldn't say. The words had come out before the thought had even registered in his brain.

"No, thank you," she said. "I'm sure I can judge for myself. Now, if you don't mind, please either put the notice up on the wall for me or hand me a hammer and I'll do it myself."

He muttered a swear word, but bent over and retrieved a hammer from under the counter. For a few seconds, he did think about posting the notice for her, then ripping it down as soon as she left, but somehow, he suspected she'd be back to check on it often.

He grabbed a nail from a bucket on his way through the store and headed to the back corner where coal oil, rope, and tools were displayed.

Two men were in the middle of a game of checkers on an upturned empty pickle barrel in front of the wall. He stopped in front of them. "Excuse me, but the lady here wants me to post a notice."

"What's she looking for?" the older of the two men asked.

"A husband."

The man slid a glance at her and gave her a toothless grin. "I ain't got a wife right now. Just buried the third one."

Devin peered at her, his brows lifting in a see-what-I-mean look. Then he turned and nailed the poster into the wall, noticing for the first time that she'd put where she was staying on the bottom. Big mistake, in his opinion.

"It's not a smart thing to do, telling the men you're staying at the boarding house."

"That may be true, but how else will they find me? I'm sure it'll be fine. Virginia and Will are there to act as chaperones."

Devin shrugged. "Suit yourself." With one hand splayed on the paper, he gripped the nail in two fingers and rested it against the notice, then hammered it into the wall. "There you are," he said. "Satisfied?"

"I am," she replied. "Thank you and good day."

He watched her wheel around and stride across the store. Why should he care if the fool woman wants to marry some sidewinder? It wasn't his problem. He had enough problems of his own to worry about. But something deep inside him had to try one more time to make her see reason. It was nothing personal. He'd feel the same no matter who was doing what she was doing. Wouldn't he?

She'd almost reached the door when Devin called her name. She turned to face him. "Yes?"

"You're going to regret this," he said. "I wish you'd change your mind."

"I'll be happy to change my mind, just as soon as you change yours."

Sybil's stomach churned as she wandered aimlessly along the boardwalk. What was she thinking, advertising for a man to spend her remaining days with? She should just go back to Ohio, back to her old life and her old friends. She had a good life there, didn't she?

No, she didn't, she admitted to herself. Her days had been filled with household chores and caring for her mother. Her mother was gone now, and what did she have to fill the void? Nothing.

Besides, Violet had assured her she'd join her in Colorado when they'd said goodbye at the train station the day she left. She couldn't wait to see her friend again, and the thought of Violet starting a new life here in Colorado with her lifted her spirits.

Devin McGregor's handsome face suddenly popped into her mind. It was a shame he wasn't interested in marriage. Even though she didn't know him, at least he was pleasant to look at. More than just pleasant, if she was being completely honest with herself. And he had been recommended by a man of the law.

It was more than his appearance that attracted her, though. Something about him, something she couldn't define, appealed to her, affected her and drew her to him like a bee to a fragrant flower.

But he'd refused, so now she had no choice but to try to find another man she didn't find too repulsive.

"Sybil!"

The voice from behind interrupted her thoughts. She spun around to see Virginia and two other ladies approaching.

"My goodness, you were miles away," Virginia said with a smile. "I called you three times."

Sybil returned her smile. "Wool-gathering, that's all."

"I'd like you to meet my friends," she said. "This is Poppy Tyler."

Sybil smiled at the woman whose hair was a mass of carrot-colored curls pinned back in a failed attempt to contain them into a bun at the nape of her neck.

"And this is Grace Morgan," Virginia went on. "She's not only the town's doctor, but my sister-in-law. Sort of."

Once Sybil greeted the women, she chuckled. "It seems Devin was right. There really are a lot of Morgans in this town, aren't there?"

"You can't go far without tripping over one of us," Grace put in with a laugh.

"Amos and Jeb have gone away for the day, and Will took Jeremy with him so I'm playing hooky. We're going for lunch at the hotel," Sybil said. "Would you like to join us?"

"Well … I don't want to intrude …"

"You're not intruding at all," Poppy said. "We'd love to have you."

Sybil grinned. "Then I accept." Perhaps spending some time with other women was what she needed to settle her nerves—and wait for suitors to come calling.

CHAPTER 5

*H*er advertisement had only been posted for two days and she'd already had four callers. Three of them were the kind of men Devin had warned her about. The third, Noah Potter, seemed nice enough, and she'd agreed to have supper with him at the hotel the next evening.

He wasn't as handsome as Devin, but she'd never been one to put much stock in a man's looks. As her mother had pointed out to her countless times, when a man is old and feeble, it doesn't matter how handsome he was when he was young. It's how a man treats a woman that matters.

Noah was prompt, which was one point in his favor, she decided. As they rode to the hotel in his buggy, he assured her he met all the qualifications she'd listed on the advertisement.

He was a gentleman, opening the door for her to

enter the hotel first and holding her chair until she sat down at the table in the dining room. He had decent table manners, too, she noticed. All in all, he was a promising candidate.

While they dined on roast chicken and potatoes, he shared his past with her. He'd grown up on a ranch in Wyoming, and had moved to Rocky Ridge a few months ago. He'd been looking for a small piece of land to buy, hoping to build it into a successful horse-breeding operation. Her notice had caught his eye.

"I assure you I know everything there is to know about ranching," he said. "I even took a ride out to your ranch this afternoon to see the size of the house."

The house? It seemed to her that he should be more interested in the land. "The house is quite large—"

"I saw that. Lots of room for children."

Children! She hadn't even thought any further ahead than a wedding. She certainly hadn't given any thought to a wedding night and the physical side of marriage.

"I have a lot of ideas for repairing the house," he went on, "and as soon as you get the cattle back from Hutchings, we can make plans for getting rid of them and buying some good horseflesh."

"I—" She'd expected … no, she'd wanted … to build the ranch back into the cattle ranch her father had loved. But she knew nothing about cattle, so she couldn't bring herself to insist on cattle rather than horses. Still, it annoyed her a little that Noah seemed to be taking control and making decisions that affected her without even consulting her.

"I'd like to get married as soon as possible," he went on.

Movement out of the corner of her eye caught her attention. She tilted her head and saw Devin at the doorway to the dining room. Her heartbeat did a little dance behind her ribs. "Good evening, Devin," she said as he came inside and approached their table.

"Evening, Sybil," he said. Then he nodded a greeting to Noah. "How are you doing, Noah?"

"I'm fine," Noah said. "What are you doing here?"

By the tone of Noah's voice and the way his eyes narrowed slightly, it was obvious to Sybil that he wasn't happy about Devin's sudden appearance, but she had no idea why.

"How's the family?" Devin asked.

Noah's face flushed, and Sybil noticed a muscle tighten in his jaw. "Fine."

"I haven't seen the little ones in the store for a few weeks," Devin continued.

Little ones? Noah hadn't mentioned having children. Of course, she hadn't asked because it hadn't occurred to her. She'd wrongfully assumed that since her suitors would be unmarried that they'd also be childless.

"Little ones?" she asked pointedly. "How many children do you have, Noah?"

One or two might be acceptable if their relationship progressed enough that she'd consider marrying him.

The slightly smug expression on Devin's face told her he'd brought up the children on purpose. He looked down at Sybil. "He didn't tell you about them? Cuter than a basket of puppies. All of them."

"All of them?" she repeated, sliding her glance back to Noah. "How many, Noah?" she asked again.

"Six."

She couldn't stop the gasp that escaped her lips. "Six? And you didn't think that was something you should have told me before I agreed to have supper with you?"

"I lost my wife last year, and since then, my children have been running wild. They need a mother. You need somebody who can run your ranch. Seemed like we could both get what we needed."

Sybil almost laughed. She might need a husband, but she certainly wasn't willing to—or even capable of —caring for six children. "I'm sorry, Noah. I sympathize with you and your children, but getting used to marriage to someone I barely know would be difficult enough. Mothering six children at the same time would be impossible for me."

She stood up and Noah made to rise. "Please don't get up. I'll walk home. Goodbye, Noah."

"And goodnight to you, Devin," she added as she turned and walked out.

Devin watched her go, her head held high and her step sure and steady. Still, he could tell by the expression on her face when she'd found out about Noah's children that she'd been disappointed.

He shouldn't have interfered, but what kind of man would he be if he'd let her get hoodwinked into a worse situation than she was in now?

He'd known Potter ever since he'd brought his children to Rocky Ridge to live with his wife's parents after she died. It hadn't taken long before his in-laws had made it clear they expected him to support his family himself.

Just a few weeks before, he'd almost convinced another woman to marry him. She'd found out about the children only by accident a few days before the wedding.

Devin suspected Noah hadn't planned to tell Sybil about them either until it was too late.

Still, he felt guilty that he'd caused her any kind of disappointment, and as he left the hotel and saw her standing in front of the milliner's window, he couldn't resist trying to make amends.

Why he felt he should, he couldn't say, but it bothered him more than it should to see her so upset because he'd refused to marry her.

Nobody would blame him for turning down her proposal, he reasoned, but if he'd agreed to marry her, she wouldn't look so forlorn right now. To cheer a woman up was no reason to get married, though. Still, if he was going to find himself a wife, he wouldn't mind waking up to a pretty woman like Sybil every morning.

As he watched, two cowboys walked past her, giving her more than a passing glance. He swore, and picked up his pace. He reached her just as one of the cowboys began to approach her. He glared at the cowboy, who shrugged and walked away.

Sybil looked up and met his gaze when he stopped beside her.

"I'm sorry about what happened back there," he said. "I didn't know he hadn't told you. I figured you were fine with becoming an instant mother."

She let out a brittle laugh. "No, he didn't tell me, and the fact that he hid something so important can't help but make me wonder what other secrets he might have hidden from me."

"I don't know much else about him," Devin told her. "Look, why don't I walk you back to the boarding house? It's starting to get dark."

"It's really not necessary—"

"I'd like to." As the words left his mouth, he realized he was telling the truth, not just saying it because making sure she got back to the boarding house safely was the right thing to do. He really did want to walk her home, wanted to talk to her, to find out why she was so determined to marry a stranger so she could keep her inheritance.

It wasn't about the money. He'd bet his boots on

that. He barely knew Sybil, but his gut told him money wasn't at the root of it.

"All right," she said, then started walking down the boardwalk toward the boarding house. "I do want to thank you. If you hadn't happened by, I have my suspicions that Noah wouldn't have mentioned the children until it was too late."

"Glad to help," he said, keeping quiet about the fact that he hadn't 'happened by', as she put it. It was none of his business who Sybil married, but when he'd found out she was having supper with Noah, he couldn't stop himself from making sure she knew about the children before she said her I-do's.

"Have you known Noah long?" she asked.

"Just a few months, since he moved to town." He took her elbow and supported her while she climbed down the steps of the boardwalk at the edge of town and rounded the corner toward the boarding house.

"When did you come to Rocky Ridge?" she asked as he released her.

"I was born and raised here."

"You never wanted to leave? To see the rest of the world?"

He shook his head. "I was happy here."

She stopped and gazed up at him. "Was?"

"I … things aren't as good as they could be right now, that's all. But I'm not complaining."

"Because you lost your ranch?"

"So you heard about that," he said.

She nodded. "But I don't know why and how you lost it."

He swore inwardly. This was getting far too personal. He wasn't about to tell her why he wasn't a rancher now, that he'd been too arrogant and stupid to listen to those who knew better than he did. "It's a long story, and it's in the past. No point rehashing it. Besides, we're here."

And not a minute too soon, Devin thought. Sybil had a way about her that made him want to open up to her, to share his innermost thoughts and feelings. And that was not a good thing.

"Oh, I hadn't even noticed," she said with a small chuckle as she opened the gate leading to the house. "Goodnight then, and thank you again."

"Any time," he said. He tipped his hat and walked away. As he made his way back to his room at the other end of town, he realized he'd meant what he'd said. Somehow, she'd gotten under his skin, something no other woman had been able to do.

But she was bound and determined to marry somebody, and he couldn't let her do that unless it was the right man.

She needed somebody to protect her from unscrupulous men who'd take advantage of her and her situation, and it looked like he'd have to be that somebody.

"It was a disaster," Sybil told Virginia over breakfast the next morning. "He didn't tell me he had six children. Six! If it hadn't been for Devin showing up unexpectedly, I would likely be engaged by now. And I'm almost positive Noah had no intention of mentioning his children. I mean, wouldn't you think that would be one of the first things you'd tell a prospective wife? Especially *six* children?"

Virginia added milk to her tea and took a sip. "I'd think so."

"I'm going back to the mercantile to change my advertisement this morning."

Devin was scooping out bags of sugar for two elderly ladies in the mercantile when she arrived, so she didn't stop to speak to him. Instead, she made her way through the store until she reached the back wall where her advertisement was posted.

She reached into her reticule and drew out a pencil, then touched the point to her tongue before she wrote "Absolutely NO Children" at the bottom of her list of requirements.

As she was finishing, Devin came to stand beside her. "I'm surprised to see you back here," he said. "Taking the notice down?"

"Heavens, no. I came to add something to it." She pointed to the latest addition she'd written on the bottom.

"You think every other man now is going to be honest?"

"I certainly hope so. Now, if you'll excuse me …"

"So you're still bound and determined to find yourself a husband this way?"

She looked up at him, again drawn into the depths of his gold-brown eyes. "Why wouldn't I?"

"I thought you might have changed your mind after what happened last night."

"Have you?"

"Why do you want me to marry you anyway? You don't even know me."

It was a reasonable question. Unfortunately, she didn't have an answer. She was attracted to him. She could admit that to herself although she'd never tell him. If she was forced to marry, she couldn't think of any other man who made her body tingle, and who she'd found herself wondering what his lips would feel like on hers. And she'd caught herself wondering just that the night before as she lay in bed trying to sleep. "You seem like a decent man, and you come highly recommended. Isn't that a good enough reason?"

"I suppose it would be," he replied, "if I was in the market for a wife. But I'm not."

"I'm also offering you a ranch. A very valuable ranch, if Mr. Morgan is to be believed. Most men wouldn't turn that down."

"I'm not most men," he pointed out. "I'm not interested in ranching. Not anymore."

"You never did tell me why you don't have your own ranch. I can't imagine you're happier working for someone else rather than being in control of your own future."

"No, I didn't tell you." His voice grew strained. "You want to know what happened, go ask anybody else in town. I don't want to talk about it."

There it was again, the sadness that seemed to fill his eyes. "Of course, I'm sorry. I shouldn't pry—"

"If you're going to keep seeing men you don't know, just be careful. There are a lot of men who'll tell you anything they think you want to hear, but they can't be trusted."

She smiled faintly and turned away. "Thank you for the advice. I'll keep it in mind."

"Good."

She looked back at him as she opened the door. "Until you change yours," she added with a grin, then walked out.

It was closing time on Saturday. Devin heaved a sigh of relief as he turned the sign on the door to "Closed" even though Reuben Day and Abner Tyler were still at the back of the store playing checkers. He'd give them a few minutes to finish their game, but he hoped it wouldn't take too long. The sun was still streaming through the window and he couldn't wait to go for a ride and breathe in some fresh mountain air.

He was restless, had been ever since Sybil had left

the store the morning before. He'd wanted to go after her and make her see that what she was doing wasn't just foolish, it could be downright dangerous. But he couldn't. What she was doing was none of his business. He had no right to interfere. She was a grown woman and could do whatever she wanted to, regardless of how he felt about it.

There was one way he could stop her. He knew that. All he had to do was agree to marry her. Not that being married to her would be the worst thing that could happen to him.

When he'd walked her back to the boarding house after her supper with Noah Potter, he'd found himself wishing they'd had farther to walk. He'd liked being with her, and he'd noticed he'd felt more relaxed with her than he'd felt in months.

But marrying her came with a whole load of respon-sibility. He couldn't even keep the small spread he'd had. How could he even think about trying to make the Franklin Ranch profitable again. No, even if he wanted to, he wouldn't risk losing her inheritance.

"I'm gonna marry her."

Abner's voice carried through the silence in the store.

Devin cringed. The thought of Abner's hands on Sybil twisted his insides into a huge knot. Jealous? How could he be jealous? He didn't want her.

"What makes you think she'd take a second look at

you when she can get any man she wants, including me?" Reuben asked.

"You?" Abner scoffed.

"Yeah, me." Reuben's voice grew louder. "I'm a sight better lookin' than you are."

"You don't know nothin' about ranching, you fool," Abner told him.

"Neither do you, but she don't have to know that. And I could sure use the money."

Devin was well aware that Reuben was broke. Just the day before, he'd asked Reuben when he planned to make a payment on the bill he owed at the store. Reuben had promised he'd take care of it that afternoon. So far, Devin hadn't seen any sign of a payment, and he'd bet next week's pay he wouldn't see it today either.

"I could use the money just as much as you," Abner pointed out. "That ranch is worth a fortune."

Devin couldn't stand listening to the two of them a minute longer. Neither one of them was good enough for Sybil, but he knew Reuben had a way with women and had managed to persuade more than one female in town to support him until she ended up as penniless as he was.

"You boys almost finished your game?" Devin asked, making his way to the back of the store. "It's closing time, so I'd appreciate it if you'd be on your way."

"Sure thing, Devin." Reuben got up. "I got some-place to go anyway."

Abner jammed his hat on his head and made for the door. "Not if I get there first."

As the two men jostled for position, trying to get through the door at the same time to get a head start toward the boarding house, Devin stood back and watched.

He could warn Sybil, but she was headstrong and probably wouldn't listen to him. He hated to admit it, but he knew all about being stubborn. He'd learned the hard way that it was usually a good idea to listen to those with knowledge and experience.

He couldn't sit back and let Abner or Reuben take advantage of her, though. Somehow, he had to stop Sybil from getting involved with either one of them.

CHAPTER 6

The knock on the door startled Sybil. She looked up from the embroidery on her lap, wondering if Abner had come back for some reason.

He'd left only a few minutes before after she'd turned down his proposal when he'd told her about his first marriage and had detailed his deceased wife's every fault. By the time he was finished, Sybil wondered if perhaps the woman had died just to get away from him.

Of course he hadn't realized how his comments had helped her to decide to turn him down.

"Can you see who that is?" Virginia's voice carried from the kitchen. "My hands are covered in flour."

Sybil threaded her needle through the linen she was working on and set it aside, then got up and crossed to the door.

A stranger stood on the porch when she opened it, his hat in his hand. "Evening, Miss Franklin," he said.

"I'm Reuben Day. I saw your notice in the mercantile and I'm here to court you, as long as it doesn't take too long. I'm not a patient man."

She supposed he could be considered attractive, although his black hair was starting to thin at the sides, and she didn't find the mustache hiding his upper lip appealing at all. His pale blue eyes held an expression she could only describe as ... cold. Still, she couldn't afford to judge his character too hastily based purely on his physical appearance. And he did seem to be agreeable to a short courtship, which was a point in his favor.

She stepped out onto the porch. "I'm pleased to meet you," she said politely. "Would you care to sit down?" She gestured toward the rocking chairs on the porch.

"Glad to," he replied, sliding into one of the chairs and resting one ankle on his opposite knee. "I don't know what you need to know about me, but I'm ready and willing to marry you whenever you say."

She perched on the edge of the other rocking chair, her hands in her lap. "I see."

"Harvey and I were friends, so I'd be honored to be the one to take care of the ranch he built. Of course, it's going be expensive to do the repairs—"

"Really?"

"Don't you worry your pretty little head about it," he said. "Once we're married, I'll handle the money and the ranch will be up and running again in no time."

It was law that her husband would have control over

their finances, but the thought of handing over her whole inheritance to someone else didn't sit well with her.

"I would like some say in how my inheritance is spent," she put in.

He waved away her comment. "I'll take care of it."

His attitude toward her inheritance niggled at her, and she couldn't help feeling he was a little too anxious to get his hands on the money that came along with the marriage license.

"Now, when do you want to tie the knot? I already asked the preacher and he can marry us tomorrow."

"Tomorrow?"

"Sure. Why not? Might as well get it done so I can start working on the ranch."

"I still have some time, and I'd like us to get to know each other a little better since I plan on this being a lifelong marriage. I also want to be sure you're qualified to rebuild my father's ranch."

"You bet I am," he said.

He smiled brightly, but it didn't quite reach his eyes, and a sense of foreboding washed over her.

"Why, I've been running ranches since I was barely old enough to rope a steer," he went on.

"Really?" Somehow, the pallor of his skin belied his claim, raising her suspicions. Shouldn't a man who spent his days outdoors have some color to his skin?

Like Devin's. The thought came unbidden into her mind. Even though he was spending his days now working at the mercantile, his skin had a sun-tinged glow which meant he spent time outside as well.

She wasn't comfortable with Reuben and was looking for a polite way to turn him down when a squeaking sound caught her attention.

She couldn't prevent the smile creasing her lips when she saw Devin opening the gate and strolling toward them. "Devin!"

"Evening, Sybil. Reuben."

Reuben nodded slightly as a greeting. "Something we can do for you?"

"Just out walking," Devin commented. "You hurried out this afternoon without making the payment you promised. It's been nigh on two months. When I saw you here, I just thought I'd ask you again when you might come by with it."

Reuben's face reddened. "I told you. Soon."

"Well," Devin said, climbing the porch steps and leaning against the railing. "Here's the thing. Elias is after me to stop giving you credit since you haven't paid anything on your account for the past two months. I don't want to do that, so if you could just pay the balance—"

Sybil's eyes widened, and it took everything Devin had to stop the smile that threatened. His plan was working.

"I'll pay it tomorrow."

"That's what you said last week. Can you pay it now and that way I won't have Elias giving me trouble."

Sybil gazed at Reuben. "You have credit at the mercantile?"

"Well … yes … everybody does …"

Sybil turned to Devin. "Is that true? Everyone has credit?"

"They do if they want it," Devin replied. "Elias is generous that way. But most folks pay regularly."

A muscle in Reuben's jaw tensed and his lips pressed into a hard line. If looks could kill, Devin would be a dead man, Sybil mused.

"You'll get your money in the morning," Reuben said. "Now we're in the middle of something here, so if you don't mind …"

Sybil stood up. "Actually, Reuben was just about to leave." She turned to him. "I'll consider your offer and let you know."

Giving Devin a glare, Reuben got up and stormed away.

"Sorry about that," Devin said when Reuben had disappeared around the corner. "I didn't mean to interfere in your courtship, but even though Reuben comes into the store almost every day, he hasn't paid his bill for months. Whenever we try to talk to him about it, he has some reason to leave in a hurry. This seemed like a good opportunity."

Sybil smiled at Devin. "I understand, and to be honest, I'm glad I found out about his financial situation before I seriously considered marrying him. I can't afford to have my inheritance squandered when there's so much to be done at the ranch to bring it back to a profitable business."

"Do you know what needs to be repaired and what kind of costs you're looking at?"

She shook her head. "I wish I did. It would be so much easier to make plans if I knew what kind of expenses I'll have."

"I'd be happy to go out there with you and take a look," Devin said.

Sybil couldn't contain her surprise—or her happiness—that she was going to spend the day with Devin. "Really? That would be wonderful. When?"

"Oh … well … what about tomorrow? The store isn't open on Sundays."

"That would be perfect."

"Then I'll come around right after church and we can head out."

Sybil watched him walk away a few minutes later, a smile tugging at her lips. Perhaps he was coming around. Why else would he be interested in helping her? And perhaps, if she could somehow arrange to spend more time with him, she could convince him to change his mind.

The chill had left the early morning air and the sun was beaming down by the time Devin drew the buckboard to a stop in front of the boarding house.

Sybil was sitting in one of the rocking chairs on the front porch. Lord, she was pretty, he thought as he climbed down and opened the gate. He returned the smile she gave him when he walked up the path.

She got to her feet and picked up a basket from the floor beside her, then draped a blanket over her arm.

"What's this?" he asked, his gaze landing on the basket.

Her eyes sparkled with merriment. "Lunch."

"Lunch?"

"Fried chicken, potato salad, biscuits, and some of Virginia's cherry pie for dessert. I thought it would be nice to stop and have a picnic. "

He hadn't been on a picnic in … he couldn't really remember ever going on a picnic. His folks weren't the picnic type. Food was to be eaten as quick and quiet as possible so they could get back to work. Relaxing and enjoying a meal wasn't something he knew anything about.

And spending more time than he had to with Sybil wasn't a smart thing to do. Everything about her tempted him to change his mind about marrying her.

At some point during the night, he'd figured out the real reason he was poking into her business. He wanted her. He wanted to taste her lips. Wanted to feel her skin beneath his touch. Wanted to make love to her. And he hated himself for even thinking about any of that.

But the joy in her expression when she looked at

him made it impossible to refuse her something as simple as a picnic. "Sounds nice."

"It's so beautiful here," she commented as they left the town behind a short time later and followed the rutted trail toward the Triple M and the Franklin Ranch. "So different from Ohio. Have you ever been east?"

He shook his head. "Got to Missouri once, but that's as far as I've been. Have no inclination to go back there, either. I'm happy here. Can't imagine living anywhere else."

"I'm not surprised. The scenery is spectacular."

He nodded in agreement, his eyes scanning the mountains rising in the distance, the wildflowers dotting the fields and the clear blue sky.

They rode in silence for a few minutes, but Devin was uncomfortably aware of her sitting so close to him. He breathed in her scent, a lavender perfume that both soothed him and excited him at the same time. With every bump, she brushed against his thigh and even through the thick fabric separating them, her warmth stole into him, making his thoughts stray. He swore inwardly.

He couldn't let himself think about her, about what his future could be like with her as his wife. He liked her, more than he wanted to or expected to, he admitted to himself. And because of that, he couldn't be the one who caused her to lose everything.

But the alternatives … He knew the men who'd approached her and the thought of her being married to any one of them was driving him crazy and had kept him awake most of the night.

When they reached the entrance to the Franklin Ranch—little more than two posts with a sign dangling between them—he turned off the trail.

"This sure is a pretty stretch of land," he said, his gaze studying the corrals and the grazing land beyond.

"It is, and that's part of the reason I want to keep it." Her voice was soft, and her eyes held a tinge of wistfulness.

"Getting married just to keep a piece of dirt …" He let the sentence die.

"Marriages have been built on that basis for centuries," she countered. "Alliances between families, arranged marriages to end feuds, for financial stability—"

He held up his hands in mock surrender. "All right," he said with a chuckle. "You've made your point."

"And some of those marriages became love matches in the end," she added. "I'm hoping my husband and I fall madly in love eventually."

Devin's chest tightened. He wanted her to be happy, but he didn't want her to be happy with another man. He felt the frown creasing his forehead. What was he thinking?

"Doesn't look too bad from here," he said, changing the subject as he drew back on the reins in front of the house. The horses stopped and he set the brake. "The garden's overgrown, but that's easy enough to take care of."

They continued to ride around the ranch, Devin climbing down from the wagon several times to check the soil, and study the grass and weeds that grew along the fence lines.

He was about to turn and drive back toward the house when Sybil grabbed his arm. "Stop!"

He drew on the reins. "What is it?"

"Look over there," she said, pointing to a tree near a stream that ran through the field. Beneath it, he noticed a weathered wooden cross and a mound of rocks.

"I wonder if that's my father's grave."

He shrugged. "Could be. Do you want to go and see?"

"Do you mind stopping?"

"Not at all."

Devin drew the wagon to a stop, then climbed out and helped Sybil down. He watched as she picked her way through the grass toward the tree. He followed, staying a few steps behind, until she stopped beside the marker.

She turned, her expression somber. "It is," she said, then turned away from him and lowered her head. Even though he was a few feet away, he could still hear the words she spoke.

"I don't even know what to call you," she said. "Father? Papa? Pa? And I don't know why you left everything you owned to me and not Mother, and I don't know why you insisted I be married, too, but I'm sure you had your reasons. I'm doing my best to fulfill your wishes, but if I fail, I hope you know I tried my best and that I'm sorry I couldn't be a real daughter to you."

Blinking back tears, she rested her hand on the cross and ran her fingers along the engraving before turning back toward Devin.

He closed the gap between them and took her hand in his as they walked back to the wagon.

A half hour later, he stopped the wagon in front of the house. After he climbed down, he tied the reins around a hitching post and then rounded the wagon to help Sybil down.

His hands spanned her waist as he lifted her to the ground, and even though he knew he should release her, his hands wouldn't obey his brain. Heat swirled through him, settling low. His breathing quickened, and her lips beckoned him like an oasis to a man dying of thirst in the desert.

She gazed up at him, her eyes studying his face. Her lips parted slightly, a faint flush coloring her cheeks. He was mesmerized. If he didn't release her right now, he might be lost.

"Do you want to kiss me?" Her soft voice penetrated the fog that had taken over his brain.

"What?" Her hands splayed across his chest, her heat searing him.

"Do you want to kiss me?" she asked again. "Just so you know, I wouldn't mind."

Right then, he wanted nothing more than to wrap his arms around her and feel the softness of her lips against his. If he did, though, he knew he'd never be the same. One kiss wouldn't be enough. And then what? She'd go off and marry somebody else and he'd be left to relive those few moments for the rest of his life.

But if he didn't, he'd regret it for the rest of his life.

What was he supposed to do? He was damned if he did, damned if he didn't. As the thought raced through his brain, he knew there was only one decision he could make.

CHAPTER 7

Sybil's breath caught in her throat as Devin's mouth lowered to hers until their lips were almost touching. And then they were.

He kissed her, the touch of his lips soft, grazing hers as if he was waiting to see if she was going to push him away.

She didn't. She made a small whimper in her throat and her whole body turned to liquid as she gave herself up to the sudden surge of heat flowing through her veins.

She'd never been kissed before and the sensation was so exquisite she thought she might swoon.

She thought she felt Devin's thundering heartbeat through the thin fabric of her dress. Or was it hers?

Devin made a sound deep in his throat. His tongue traced the seam of her lips. She parted them, not exactly sure what he wanted from her. A moment later, his tongue swept the inside of her mouth until it tangled with hers.

Her fingers clutched at his shirt. She was unable to think, to breathe. Only feel and respond.

Her yearning increased, but for what, she didn't know. All she knew was that she wanted more … something. A heaviness settled low in her core, a need that grew with every passing second as his tongue moved in a sensual dance inside her mouth.

She'd never experienced passion before. Now she understood the kind of hunger she'd only heard about, a hunger that made her powerless in Devin's arms.

His lips left her mouth and burned a fiery trail to the hollow at the base of her neck.

"Oh … Devin …"

He froze, then pulled away and took a step back, his breathing ragged, his gaze intense.

Mercy! What must he think of her now? That she was a loose woman with no morals whatsoever. And if he'd even been considering her proposal at all, she was sure she'd destroyed any chance of it now.

Humiliation at the way she'd responded to him overwhelmed her. Her face flamed. Perhaps if she ignored it, as if the kiss had never happened … She turned away, taking in deep calming breaths until her heartbeat returned to normal.

"Sybil—"

Her voice quivered. "Some of the fences will need

to be repaired, I expect. The barn appears quite sound, though, don't you think?"

"Seems like you don't want to talk about it and that's okay, but you need to know I didn't intend for that to happen. That's not why I offered to bring you out here."

"I know." She nodded, hoping the slight acknowledgement would be enough to stop him pursuing the matter any further.

"I'll check out the barn now if you want to wait here."

"Fine." She needed time to get her emotions back under control, because the moment their lips met, she'd fallen just a little bit in love with him.

How could she marry another man now?

She wouldn't think about that now, she decided. She was here with Devin to take a close look at the house and outbuildings, to see what costs she could expect to restore them.

While he went to the barn, Sybil walked around the side of the house. She'd noticed the small vegetable garden when Brett had brought her to the ranch, but now, she studied it more closely. Her father had planted tomatoes, beans, potatoes and corn, all of the plants dead now.

She'd had a small plot back in Ohio, but here, there was enough space here that she could expand it and plant enough vegetables and berries to last an entire year.

She was planning what vegetables she'd put in the next spring when she heard footsteps and turned in time to see Devin climb the porch steps and open the front door of the house. She followed behind.

Spiders and other creatures had taken up residence in the house, but it was easy to see that the room would be bright and airy once it was cleaned. A stone fireplace filled one wall, and for a few seconds, Sybil stood quietly picturing a roaring fire and her father sitting in the armchair reading the book still on the table beside it.

A doorway led to a large kitchen with a long oak table and chairs filling the center. Stairs led from the corner of the kitchen to a second floor, matching the stairs rising from the main room as well to the bedrooms.

"Nice house," Devin muttered, coming to stand beside her.

"It is," she agreed.

"The barn's solid, too. Needs cleaned up but otherwise, not much work to be done in there."

"Good." She turned and crossed to the stairs leading to the second floor. Devin followed.

A flush rose in Sybil's cheeks when she entered each of the bedrooms with Devin behind her. Her eyes seemed to focus on the beds, and she couldn't help wondering if Devin felt as uncomfortable as she did.

Hurrying through her inspection, she went downstairs and waited until he joined her. "What do you think about the house?"

"There's a few loose boards on the porch and the whole house could use paint, but it'll be livable once you get rid of the critters who've moved in."

She shuddered at the thought of dealing with spiders, mice, and Heaven knew what other creatures were living there, but if she wanted to live in the house, she'd have to put her fears aside.

"So to get the ranch up and working again, it's mainly fencing that's broken and hay that needs to be put up for the winter," he told her. "The rest can be done gradually."

"How much will it cost to fix all this?"

"Not as much as you'd think. It's more hard work than money."

"Reuben said it would be expensive, but I suspect he was more interested in getting his hands on my inheritance than in rebuilding the ranch" she commented.

He smiled at her, and her heart fluttered in her chest. What was it about this man that had such an effect on her?

"I'm glad you figured out what Reuben was up to," he said. "I hope you're as careful with any other man who comes around."

"I will be," she promised. "Now, are you hungry? Ready for our picnic?"

He nodded. "The smell of that fried chicken has been making my stomach grumble since we left town."

"Good. If you'll get the basket, I'll set the blanket under those trees," she said, pointing through the window to a stand of weeping willows near a small pond at the back of the house.

Devin relaxed against the trunk of a young willow whose branches shaded him and Sybil but didn't yet reach the ground. A soft breeze rustled the leaves, the scent of pine and cedar from the trees nearby drifting in the air.

He'd eaten his fill and now he was quite content to look out over the meadow to the mountain ridges rising to the clear blue sky. He slid a glance in Sybil's direction as she cleared away the remnants of their meal. "It's real pretty right here," he said. He didn't mention that the pretty scenery he was talking about also included her.

"Now do you understand why I want to keep it?"

"I suppose I do," he replied. "I mean, it's valuable land, and you'll be a rich woman—"

"It's not about the value of the land," she said.

A lot of women might say that, but they'd be lying. His gut told him that Sybil was telling the truth, that money didn't mean much to her.

"It's about building a new life, a life I wish I'd known about. It's about a father I didn't get the chance to know, to continue what he started, to be closer to him. Did you know him?"

Devin thought back to the man who'd apparently

deserted his wife and daughter years before. He still found it hard to believe. "I did," he said.

"What was he like?"

"Big. Loud. Appreciated a good joke. Kind, but tough and unforgiving if somebody crossed him. Loyal to a fault."

"I wish I'd known him."

"You don't know why he left you and your mother?"

Sybil shook her head. "I hoped there'd be a clue in the letters, but he never mentioned it, and my mother always led me to believe he'd died when I was a baby. I suppose she did that so I wouldn't question why he left us."

"He spoke about you and your mother often," he told her. "How he hoped he'd see you again one day. I still find it strange that he'd put you in a position of having to marry somebody you don't even know ..." The words trailed off as a vision of Sybil wrapped in another man's arms filled his mind. His stomach tightened and his teeth clenched at the thought.

"I have no choice if I want to stay." Her voice lowered. "You probably think I'm being stupid."

He sat up straighter and shifted so he could look at her squarely. "I do *not* think you're stupid, but I *do* think that what you're doing is ..."

"Is what? Foolish? "

"I was going to say it's risky, possibly dangerous."

"I took a risk coming all the way out here instead of staying in Ohio."

Devin watched the play of emotions on her face and the way the sun glimmered on the reddish-gold strands in her dark hair. "It must have been hard to give up your life there."

"What life? I spent my life caring for my mother. Not that I resent that. I don't. But she's gone now, and I had nothing else there. It was time to live my life."

"And you're willing to take the risks that come with that?"

She gazed at him for a moment, then spoke quietly. "Isn't everything we do in life risky? Even something as simple as walking along a street is risky. A fall? A runaway wagon? A stray bullet? I refuse to go through life being afraid of what *might* happen."

Devin supposed she was right. "You are without a doubt the bravest woman I've ever met."

"Not brave," she countered. "Desperate."

She *was* desperate, and that worried Devin more than he wanted to admit. "Desperation is the worst time to make a life-changing decision."

"I realize that," she said, "but since you don't want—"

He shook his head. "I can't."

As the words left his mouth, he realized that it wasn't that he didn't want to marry her. Lord help him, he did. Because somehow, even though he'd been fighting it since she'd walked into his store that day, she'd managed to get under his skin, and he was afraid he was falling in love with her.

And that would be the worst thing that could ever happen to him. Because loving Sybil would force him to choose—between her and his fear of failure.

Sybil paced the main room in the boarding house, her teeth nibbling on her bottom lip. "I'm running out of time, Virginia," she said. "I only have three days left and not one suitable man has come calling." She'd turned away two prospective husbands in the past few days and it seemed there wasn't one man in town she'd be willing to marry.

Well, she amended, there was *one* man, but he wasn't willing to marry her.

Virginia poured her a cup of tea from a patterned china teapot. "I wish I could help, but—"

"I know." Sybil sent a wan smile in Virginia's direction. "Perhaps I'm being too particular. I'm looking for the perfect husband, and there likely isn't such a man. Loren Smith invited me to go walking with him this afternoon. I accepted even though I'd rather not."

"I don't think Loren is the right man for you."

"I agree, but if he's my only option, I'll have to marry him if he offers."

"I'm sure you'll find someone else."

"Why don't you sound convinced?" Sybil asked wryly.

"Come and have some tea and cookies. Tea always makes me feel better when I have a problem."

Sybil slipped into a chair and dropped a cube of sugar into her tea. Stirring absently, her thoughts drifted to the man she'd promised to spend the afternoon with. He was certainly big enough and strong enough to handle the hard work on a ranch. He'd assured her he had no debts and no children.

Yet something in his manner frightened her a little, although she couldn't say why. But as she'd said to Virginia, he might be her only choice.

CHAPTER 8

*L*oren's deep voice rattled her eardrums. "As long as you're able to share my bed, we'll get along just fine. I have needs and I expect my wife to take care of those needs whenever and wherever I choose."

Sybil sucked in a gasp. This was highly improper. That he would even mention the intimate side of marriage to a woman he'd just met … and to be so blunt about his expectations … For the first time in her life, she found herself speechless.

They'd been walking for only a few minutes along Rocky Ridge's main street when he'd stopped in mid-stride. He'd turned to look down at her, his expression intense. Then he'd made this announcement.

In fact, since they'd left the boarding house, she'd barely had a chance to speak at all. He'd dominated the conversation, informing her in a stern tone what the rules and expectations would be once they were married.

That was not going to happen. She wouldn't spend even one more day with this … brute!

A few minutes with him and it was plain to see why he wasn't already married. What woman in her right mind would agree to such terms?

Finally, when it seemed he'd stopped talking long enough to take a breath, she spoke. "Well … I … before I discuss that aspect of marriage—"

"I'll be the man of the house, and I'll expect obedience," he went on as if she hadn't spoken at all. "Without question."

For the first time since she'd arrived in Rocky Ridge, Sybil admitted to herself that she'd go back to Ohio rather than marry this … egotistical oaf.

The thought crossed her mind that she should turn around and go back to the boarding house right this minute. There was no point in prolonging her misery since at the end of their walk, she'd be telling him in no uncertain terms that there would be no wedding.

But they were close to the mercantile and she couldn't help hoping she might see Devin, even a glimpse through the window. It was silly. She knew that. He filled her thoughts and her dreams these days, and somehow, during their afternoon together, she'd fallen in love with him.

He didn't love her. He didn't want to marry her. But that didn't stop her wishing and hoping and dreaming that one day, he'd reconsider and they'd spend the rest of their lives together on the ranch.

She'd felt a change in their relationship that day, but it hadn't been enough to make him change his mind about marrying her. On the way back to town, she'd asked him to stop at the mercantile so she could add "debt free" to her advertisement.

The mood had changed at that moment and he'd grown quiet during the rest of the drive. They'd stopped at the mercantile and she'd changed the notice, then he'd taken her back to the boarding house.

For a few seconds when his hands spanned her waist to help her out of the buggy, she'd thought he might kiss her again. But he hadn't. He'd released her as if she'd been a flame, then grabbed the basket and blanket and carried it up to the porch.

With a muttered goodbye, he'd hurried away, leaving her standing, watching as he drove away.

She hadn't seen him since, and it seemed whenever she went to the mercantile now, Elias or his daughter, Cammie, were manning the counter.

She'd heard he was living in a room in the back of the livery stable now that Landry Mitchell, the blacksmith, had married, and she'd thought about going to see him on some pretense. But she'd resisted. Their kiss had apparently meant nothing to him.

She'd even been tempted to ask about Devin the last time she was in the mercantile but had thought better of it. No point in giving the gossips in town any more reasons than they already had to talk about her and her situation.

"We'll walk to the end of the street, then turn back." Loren's voice interrupted her thoughts. "Then we'll get this settled once and for all."

They certainly would, she thought.

As they passed the mercantile, she cast a glance at the window, tamping down her disappointment when she didn't see Devin behind the counter.

Suddenly, the door burst open. Devin appeared in the entrance a moment before a cloud of dust, dirt and debris exploded in the air, landing on Loren and clinging to his shaggy hair and his clothes.

"Oh … sorry, Loren …" Devin was holding a broom in one hand, a dustpan in the other. His voice was contrite, but Sybil couldn't help noticing a distinct gleam in his eye that made her wonder if he hadn't arranged his timing perfectly, and tossed the contents of the dustpan on Loren on purpose.

Loren's face, on the other hand, had reddened and was mottled with anger. His eyes darkened and glittered with hatred when he looked in Devin's direction. His hands clenched into fists and before Sybil knew what was happening, he let out a loud curse, raised his fist and punched Devin squarely in the nose.

"Ohhh," Sybil cried out on a gasp of shock and horror, her hands steepling over her mouth.

The blow from Loren's fist threw Devin off balance. He reeled, letting go of the dustpan and broom, his arms flailing in the air. There was nothing within reach to stop him falling.

He crashed to the floor, his head smacking into the wall. Blood spurted from a cut on his cheek and from his nose.

Loren swore again, his voice booming as he brushed the dust and dirt off this shirt. He didn't seem concerned at all that he'd injured Devin. He gave Devin one last look, then he gripped Sybil's elbow and tried to lead her away. "Let's go."

Sybil shook herself loose from his grasp. "No. I'm not going anywhere with you."

"I said—" He made a move as if he was going to force her to go with him, but she stepped out of his reach.

"Leave. Now. Otherwise I will call the sheriff and have you arrested for assault."

Loren glared at her for what seemed like hours, but she stared him down. Finally, he turned and stalked off.

A crowd was gathering around them. Sybil hurried back to Devin's side. Blood dripped from his nose, spattering the white apron he was wearing over his shirt. "Come inside and let me take care of that for you."

"It's fine," he muttered, but by the pallor of his skin and the muscle pulsing in his jaw, she could tell he was in pain.

"I insist."

As if he was too weak to argue, he gingerly got to his feet. Tucking her hand beneath his elbow, she steered him back into the mercantile and locked the door behind her.

Devin's head was spinning from the goose-egg he could already feel on the back of his head. His nose and cheek hurt like the devil, but it had been worth it to keep Sybil out of Loren Smith's clutches.

The man was a bully through and through, and any woman who got mixed up with him was likely to end up with more than the black eye Devin figured he be sporting come morning.

Devin sat on a chair in the mercantile storeroom watching Sybil as she scurried around collecting fresh water from a pitcher on the table and clean cloths from a bureau against the far wall.

She set the bowl of water on the table beside him and dampened a cloth. "Hold this against your nose," she ordered, handing him the cloth.

Then she leaned over him, her fingers carefully parting his hair to examine the bump, her breasts coming far too close to him for comfort.

It was taking all his concentration to control himself when all he wanted to do was to wrap his arms around her, draw her down into his lap and kiss her senseless.

Then she moved away and took the blood-soaked cloth from his hand. He sucked in a relieved breath, but his relief was short-lived.

"Hold still," she ordered.

She dabbed the cloth gently against the blood already starting to dry on his face. Even though his nose throbbed, he apparently wasn't in enough pain for his body to ignore her touch, shards of heat snaking through his veins and settling low in his belly every time her fingers grazed his skin.

When she was finished, her gaze focused on his nose for a few seconds. For the first time, he noticed a tiny scar near her ear, but before he had a chance to ask her about it, she straightened. "The bleeding seems to have stopped," she said, "but I'm sure it'll be painful for a few days."

"I expect so."

She straightened and moved away until her back came into contact with the wall. Facing him, she folded her arms across her chest. "I don't understand how it is that you seem to show up every time I'm interviewing—"

His brows lifted. "Interviewing? This isn't an employee you're hiring. This is a man you're going to spend your life with." And share a bed with, he wanted to add but thought better of it. The subject wasn't one a man talked about with a woman unless they were already married.

"Don't change the subject," she went on. "It's as if you're trying to stop me from finding a husband."

"Why would I want to do that?" he asked, even though he was well aware of the answer he wasn't about to voice. The truth of the matter was that he couldn't marry her himself, but he couldn't stand the thought of her married to any other man.

He was falling in love with her—her beauty, her spirit, even her stubbornness that was going to get her into serious trouble. And even though her leaving would destroy him, he'd rather see her go back to Ohio than married to the wrong man.

"My question precisely," she said. "While I appreciate you rescuing me from Noah and his children, and pointing out Reuben's money problems—"

"You forgot to mention me saving you from Loren Smith's temper tantrums," he put in, trying to smile even though his cheek was starting to feel as if it had grown to twice its size.

"That's true. You did. And I suspect your need to throw out the dirt at that precise moment was no accident."

He didn't deny it.

"If you don't want to marry me, why are you trying to prevent me from finding a man who will? I only have a few days left."

"It's not that," he said. "I can't marry you."

Confusion shone in her eyes. "What did you say?"

"I can't," he repeated, more for himself than for her to hear. Then he bounded to his feet. "Thanks for your help. My nose is fine. I'd better get back to work."

Ignoring him, she moved to block the entrance between the storeroom and the store. "Why not?"

"Because …"

"Because what?"

Maybe it was time to tell her the truth. Maybe then she'd stop asking him to marry her. "I'm sure Brett told you about me," he said. "I had a ranch. It was small but I had big plans. I had everything I wanted. And I lost it."

Her brows arched. "Brett didn't tell me anything," she said softly. "Please tell me what happened."

It was common knowledge that because he hadn't listened to Cade Morgan, he'd ended up losing his livestock, and then his land.

But what nobody else knew was how those few weeks had destroyed his confidence, had turned him into a man who was so afraid of failing again that he couldn't bring himself to even try.

It surprised him that nobody had told her his story, but he was sure that once she heard about his failure, she'd be glad he'd turned her down so that he couldn't lose her ranch, too.

"Cade Morgan was my best friend from the time he came to Rocky Ridge to live with his kin," he began. "I lived in town and he lived out on the Triple M, but I used to ride out there every chance I got. The Morgans welcomed me like I was one of their own, and I knew I wanted a place just like that when I grew up." He paused, his mind drifting back to the day he'd bought his own spread—the plans he'd made, the dreams he'd had, the future he'd wanted stretching out in front of him.

"Finally, I bought my own spread. For two years, I spent every waking minute working to build my herd. I grew crops on some of the pasture land to sell to buy more cattle. I'd found the woman I wanted to marry and I was building a house for us. Everything was going my way."

"And then?"

"One of the steers got sick. Cade happened to come by and I told him what was happening. He told me to separate the steer from the herd in case it was contagious. I thought he was being over-cautious so I didn't rush to do what he suggested. He was right, and I was too late. Within a few days, I'd lost my whole herd. I had no cattle to take to market. The bank called in my note, and my future wife left me for the bank manager who foreclosed on me."

"I'm so sorry, but you didn't know—"

"I should have listened to him," he insisted. "I spent so much time at the Triple M growing up that I thought I knew ranching as well as he did. And because I was too big for my britches, it cost me everything I had."

"Can you be sure you wouldn't have been too late anyway even if you'd separated the cow as soon as your friend told you to?"

He shrugged. He hadn't really considered that possibility. Not that it changed anything. He should have recognized the symptoms, and he hadn't. But if he was being completely honest with himself, he'd feel a lot better if he knew it wasn't his hesitation that had caused his whole herd to perish. "It doesn't matter whether or not it was too late. I can't risk it again. What if something else happened and I lost everything again? Something else that I think I know but I don't?"

"You can't go through life with 'what if'," she pointed out, "because the day will come when you're old and you look back and you realize you also missed the 'what ifs' that could have made your life amazing."

Devin didn't want to think about that, didn't want to think about the possibilities if he let himself take another chance, to let himself accept Sybil's proposal.

"What happened?" Elias's booming voice bounced off the walls. Then, noticing Sybil for the first time, his eyes narrowed. "What's going on here?"

"Mr. Todd," Sybil said. "Devin was my knight in shining armor and saved me from a fate worse than death."

A little overboard, Devin thought, but he couldn't help grinning at the way Elias suddenly calmed down. "Well … I'm glad to see he was of service to you …"

"Now, if you'll lend me a pencil, I'd like to make a small addition to the advertisement I have on the wall."

"Why, certainly," Elias gushed. "Anything I can do to help."

While Elias rummaged through a drawer and found a pencil, Sybil sidled closer to Devin. Then, standing on her tiptoes to reach his ear, she whispered, "I'm willing to take the chance. The offer still stands."

A few seconds later, she took the pencil from Elias

and with an encouraging smile at Devin over her shoulder, strolled to the back of the store and disappeared from his line of sight.

Depression shrouded Sybil like a thick blanket. "It's no use, Virginia. I've almost run out of time."

Virginia picked up the rolling pin and began to roll out the pastry for the apple pies she was baking for dessert while Sybil peeled and cored the apples. "Don't give up hope."

Sybil gave her a wan smile. She knew Virginia was trying to cheer her up, but with every chime of the grandfather clock near the fireplace, her spirits sank even lower. "If I'm not married in two days, I'll miss the deadline. So, unless I marry the next man who knocks at the door no matter how repulsive he is, I'll lose the ranch. I haven't found one man who I could stand to spend the next week with, never mind the rest of my life." That wasn't exactly true, but she wasn't ready to share the fact that she'd fallen in love with the one man she'd be happy to marry, but who didn't want to marry her.

"None of the men who've been willing to marry me have met my requirements," she added. "Am I being too particular?"

"You have to be particular," Virginia pointed out. "After all, your inheritance is at stake, not to mention your happiness. Spending a lifetime with the wrong man … well, I can't imagine how dreadful that would be."

"It would," Sybil agreed. "If only I'd known … I still don't understand why my mother kept it from me, especially since she saved all his letters. There are so many questions that I'll never have answers for. What could have been so terrible that it drove them apart in the first place?"

"Maybe one day you'll find out," Virginia said hopefully. "In the meantime, there's nothing you can do except wait."

Sybil nodded. Waiting was something she'd never been very good at. When she decided she wanted something, she did whatever she needed to do to get it. Only this time, she couldn't. She had no control, and it rankled her.

Sybil scooped up the apples and put them in the pie plate lined with pastry. "There's nothing I can do. If I haven't found the perfect husband by tomorrow, I may as well start packing and buy a ticket on the stage back to Denver."

As she climbed the stairs to her room, she made one final decision about her life here in Rocky Ridge. Before she left town, she'd go to Devin and tell him exactly how she felt about him and what he was throwing away.

*H*ow many more nails can I weigh before I lose my mind? Devin wondered

as he took yet another paper bag off the scale and folded the top to close it.

Elias had come up with the idea of packaging supplies in different weights to save time when the customers were in the store, but Devin was convinced it was nothing more than something to keep Devin busy since he was being paid to work.

He paused and looked through the window to the street. Two women passed by, smiling at something he couldn't hear. That was all it took to turn his thoughts to Sybil—her smile, her chocolate eyes, her hair he wanted to feel beneath his fingers.

He loved her, more than life itself. But the one thing she'd asked him for was the one thing he couldn't give her. Because he was too scared. If he failed her, she'd hate him, and he'd rather she was angry with him than look on him with contempt.

He swore at the empty store just as the door opened and Curly strode inside. "Afternoon, Devin," he said, passing by where Devin was digging a tin scoop into a bucket of nails and continuing on to the rear of the store..

Devin filled the bag, closed it and set it aside, then followed Curly. He found the man reading Sybil's advertisement.

Curly turned when Devin stopped beside him and peered at the black and purple bruises around Devin's eyes. "Looks good," he said sarcastically, grinning.

"What can I do for you?" Devin asked, ignoring the comment.

"Came into pick up the wire Cade ordered a few weeks back. Is it in yet?"

"It is. I'll just go get it."

"I'll pick it up later," Curly said. "Heard about the lady Loren was with, too, that she's looking for a husband. I'm heading over to get me a hot bath, a shave and a haircut, and then I'm going over to the boarding house and see if she'll accept me."

Devin's heart lurched and his stomach tightened. Curly and Sybil? Married? "You?"

Curly's brow creased in a frown and his eyes narrowed. "Why not me? You don't think I'm good enough for her?"

"I didn't mean that," Devin said. "Just didn't think you were looking for a wife is all."

"Any man'd have to be a damn fool not to jump at the chance to own a spread like the Franklin place even if it does mean getting married. Saw her at the hotel the other day having lunch with Virginia Morgan and some other ladies. She's easy enough on the eyes that she'll make a good blanket companion, if you know what I mean."

Devin muttered a response and turned his back on Curly, storming back to the scale and making a bigger production out of filling more paper bags with nails.

"I'll be back later to get that wire," Curly said.

Devin heard Curly's boots clomping on the floor but he didn't turn around until the door closed behind him.

Curly and Sybil. For once, he couldn't come up with one character flaw of Curly's he could warn her about. Curly was a hard worker, honest as the day was long and a genuinely good man.

Sybil would accept Curly's proposal. There wasn't one good reason not to. It had been easy to point out the flaws in the men who'd been interested in her—the children, the debt, the temper. But there wasn't one thing he knew about Curly that would be enough to stop a woman from marrying him if she wanted to.

She'd scolded him for dwelling on 'what-if', but he was going to think about it one more time. He could fail again, but what if he didn't? What if Sybil was right, and by being too afraid to try, he might be missing out on an amazing life? What if she loved him as much as he loved her?

He had a choice—either move past his fear of failure and take the chance she offered him, or lose her. And really, he had no choice. Losing Sybil to another man would destroy him.

There was only one way to stop her, and to do that, he had to get to the boarding house before Curly did.

Sybil closed the latch on the trunk and gazed around the room she'd come to think of as hers. She'd miss being in this house, miss Virginia's friendship. She let out a short laugh. Much as she'd never thought she'd ever think it, she'd even miss Jeb and Amos, uncouth though they were. A wave of sadness washed over her, and she felt tears threaten.

Suddenly, she heard a soft knock at the door. "Sybil?"

Startled, she spun around, blinking her tears back as she crossed the room and opened the door.

"You have a visitor," Virginia said. "It's Curly Ames. He's the foreman at Cade's ranch. We've known him for years. He'd make a good husband."

"That's … good." She should be thrilled that a man Virginia and Will had high praise for was interested in her. So why wasn't she? Why did she have a sick feeling in her stomach, as if she was about to make a huge mistake.

Quickly, she tucked a stray strand of hair back into the chignon and hurried out of the room, hurrying down the stairs to the parlor.

A man with a thick head of light brown hair and sun-bronzed skin stood facing her, a worn Stetson in his hands.

"Ma'am," he said politely. "My name's Curly Ames and I'm here about your advertisement."

Sybil held out her hand. "I'm pleased to meet you, Mr. Ames. Please sit down."

"If it's all the same to you, I'll stand."

"That's fine." She took a seat on the edge of the sofa and looked up at him. He was pleasant enough to look at, and the tiny lines at the corners of his eyes led her to believe he laughed often. That was a good sign.

"I heard you need to get yourself married by day after tomorrow."

"That's right."

"Well, then," he said, then cleared his throat, "I'd be pleased if you'd do me the honor of becoming my wife."

Before she had a chance to respond, he went on. "I read everything you said you wanted, and there's a lot of folks in town who'll vouch for me. If you want, I'll go get them right now—"

"That's not necessary. Virginia and Will told me you're more than qualified."

"I don't smoke or drink, and I'm pretty handy around the house, too."

She smiled. "That's good to know."

"I'll admit I'm hoping we'll get to maybe loving each other one day, but in the meantime, I'd really like it if we could be friends. So, what do you say?"

This was it! This was that moment her whole future hinged on. All she had to do was say yes.

And she couldn't do it.

Because her heart belonged to Devin. It likely had since the first moment she'd seen him, and always would.

Curly seemed like a nice man. He had no obvious faults, and Virginia had nothing but kind words to say about him. He wanted a woman who might love him one day, and he deserved that. She wasn't that woman.

If she rejected Curly's proposal, she'd lose her inheritance and she'd have to go back to Ohio. Well, she amended, she didn't *have* to go back to Ohio, but she couldn't stay in Rocky Ridge, loving Devin from afar, knowing he didn't love her back.

What was she going to do?

Elias was going to be furious when he found out Devin had closed the store early, but Devin didn't care. He had far more important things to think about right now, like getting to the boarding house and telling Sybil he'd been wrong.

He'd realized that because he'd failed once didn't mean he'd fail again. He was ready to take a chance again, and he wanted to take that chance with her beside him. As her husband.

Rounding the corner, he noticed movement on the porch of the boarding house.

Sybil and Curly were standing on the porch. Curly was holding Sybil's hand.

His stomach clenched and his chest tightened until it was hard to breathe.

He was too late.

Mrs. Lundstrom was waiting at the mercantile door the next morning when Devin arrived. She squinted up at him through her spectacles. "You're late."

"Sorry," he replied, turning the key in the lock and opening the door. He stepped aside to allow her to enter first, then turned the sign to show the store was open.

"Are you sick, Mr. McGregor?" she asked.

If his insides feeling as if they'd been torn to shreds counted, then he was at death's door. "I'm fine, Mrs. Lundstrom. Didn't sleep well last night is all."

"Out gallivanting? Sowing your wild oats?" she pried. "You young people—"

"No. I wasn't out." He wasn't about to tell the

town's biggest gossip what he had been doing all night —thinking about Sybil and wondering how he could have been such a fool.

He didn't care about Sybil's ranch. It was a piece of dirt. Nothing more. It was the ranch's soon-to-be owner he cared about, the woman he loved and who was about to marry another man.

Today.

"… and I expect the new owner will be arriving soon from Wyoming to take possession of the Franklin ranch. It's unfortunate. I was sure Harvey's daughter would find a husband and be able to keep her father's ranch."

Mrs. Lundstrom's words dragged Devin from his thoughts. "What? What did you say?"

The woman's brows arched at the urgent tone in his voice. "Why I—"

Devin crossed to stand within inches of the woman. "What did you say about the Franklin ranch?"

She huffed out a breath. "I said that the new owner will likely be arriving soon—"

"No," he interrupted. "What did you say about Sybil?"

"That it's a shame she couldn't find a husband."

Devin came around the counter. "She did find a husband. She'll be marrying Curly Ames. And since the deadline's not until tomorrow, as long as the wedding takes place before then, she'll inherit the ranch."

Mrs. Lundstrom snickered. "If she's planning to get

married, she has a strange way of showing it. I just saw her at the Wells Fargo office waiting for the stagecoach."

How was that possible? He'd seen her and Curly together just the day before, and it sure didn't look like she'd turned him down.

And why would she? She'd been trying to find a husband since the day she arrived, and when a decent man finally offered to marry her, she refused? It didn't make sense.

"You're sure she was waiting for the stage?" he asked again. Mrs. Lundstrom was known far and wide to embellish a story.

She nodded. "It certainly looked like it, considering she was sitting outside the office on a trunk and had a valise on her lap."

Devin's heart leaped into his throat. She was leaving? That meant—

The question was, why? She'd wanted her father's ranch, and she had it in her grasp. All she had to do was marry Curly. What had happened to make her give up her inheritance and drive her away?

"Mrs. Lundstrom," he said, whipping the apron off and tossing it onto the counter. "I have to go. Help yourself to whatever you need and I'll put it on your account when I get back."

Mrs. Lundstrom's eyes widened in shock. "Well, I never—"

Devin hurried past her toward the door, then

stopped, spun around and raced to the back of the store to pluck Sybil's advertisement from the wall.

Mrs. Lundstrom hurriedly stepped out of his way before he knocked her over as he headed to the door, threw it open and ran out.

Sybil paced the boardwalk in front of the stage depot, her reticule swinging on her arm. A trunk sat against the wall, a valise on top.

She'd made the right decision, but she hadn't expected it to be so difficult to leave this town and the new friends she'd made.

But it was done. The ranch would go to her father's cousin, she'd go back to Ohio and life would go back to the way it was.

No, she amended. She'd never again be the woman she was when she left. She'd fallen in love, she'd lost. That would haunt her for the rest of her life. And one kiss would be all she'd have to remember the man she was leaving behind.

"You were going to leave without even saying goodbye?"

Startled, she spun around. Her eyes widened and her bottom lip began to tremble when she saw Devin standing there. "Devin. I … I left a note for you with Virginia. She was going to bring it to you after I left."

"You couldn't say goodbye in person?"

She shook her head. She'd thought about going to find him, but she couldn't bear to see him, to know she'd never see him again. "I thought it would be best."

"Why are you leaving?" he asked. "I figured you'd be marrying Curly."

"What made you think that?"

"He told me he was going to propose. He fit your requirements, and since you were running out of time, I figured you'd jump at the chance to get a decent man and keep your inheritance."

"I turned him down."

"Why?"

"It doesn't matter."

He took a step closer. His gaze was intense. "It matters to me."

He deserved the truth. "I realized I don't want the ranch badly enough to marry a man I don't love. Marriage is forever to me, and I knew I'd never be able to love him."

"Why not? He's a good man."

"Because …" She wanted so much to tell him how she felt about him, but the words stuck in her throat. "What are you doing here?"

"I came to stop you."

"Why?"

"Because you need to stay."

"I can't stay," she said, her voice thready. "I have nothing here."

"You told me once that I shouldn't go through life

thinking 'what if' and always looking at the worst thing that could happen."

She tried to smile but the sadness weighing her down made it impossible. "I did say that, didn't I?"

"You did. And you were right," he said. "And you said that being afraid of failure meant that I might miss out on an amazing life."

She did smile this time, through the tears that she couldn't prevent from spilling over. "I did say that, too."

The stagecoach rolled up and the driver climbed down. He stopped in front of her and tipped his hat. "Those yours?" he asked, pointing to the trunk and valise.

"They are."

"I'll be right back to load them. We'll be ready to leave in just a few minutes if you want to get settled inside."

"Thank you," she said, then turned her attention back to Devin. "I have to go—"

"Wait."

She stopped and gazed up at him. Her eyes filled with tears. "What is it?"

"You were looking for the perfect husband."

"I was, but there's no such thing."

"Let's play 'what if' just one more time. What if you're wrong?"

"I'm not wrong."

"I think you are. There might not be such a thing as

a perfect husband for everyone, but there is a perfect husband for you."

She looked up at him. "Who?"

"Me."

He handed her the advertisement with the list of qualifications penciled in. "Look at the requirements you listed. I meet them all, so you can put a check mark beside every one of them. Read the list to me."

"What?"

"Please, just read them."

"All right." She took the paper from him. "Must be between 25-35 years old."

"Twenty-eight. Check."

"Must be a hard worker."

"Check."

"Must be of sound mind and body."

He grinned. "As far as I know."

"Must have ranching experience."

He had experience, even though he'd failed in the end. But he was smarter now. "I know ranching," he began, "and I've learned to ask for help and take advice when I need it, I have no children, I'm not in debt and even though I get mad sometimes, I've never raised a hand to anybody in anger. And I swear I'd never hurt a woman."

She smiled at him. "Well, it does look like you qualify, but I knew that in the beginning when Brett recommended you. What's different now?"

"There's one more thing you forgot to add." He took

the advertisement back from her hand. Reaching into his shirt pocket, he took out a pencil and began to scribble something on the bottom before handing it back to her.

She read the words he'd written. "Must love me."

He hooked his finger under her chin and she lifted her eyes to meet his. "Check. Check and double check."

Tears welled in her eyes and rolled unheeded down her cheeks. "You mean you love me?"

He nodded. "Lord knows I didn't want to, and I tried my best not to. But I do, with every breath I take and every beat of my heart. For the first time … and probably the last … I'm really glad Mrs. Lundstrom's tongue can't stop wagging." He laughed and kissed her. "I love you, Sybil Franklin."

"You don't have to—"

"I know that. All you want is a husband, not love. But when she told me you turned Curly down and you were leaving … I thought I was too late."

"I always wanted love," she said, "but I never thought I'd be lucky enough to find a man who loved me." Her tears fell faster now, but they were tears of joy. Her heart was full.

Devin had to clear his throat before he could go on. "I want to spend the rest of my days with you, helping you to rebuild your ranch, sharing my life with you, raising a family with you. I know this is a business arrangement—"

She drew back. "But it isn't. I love you. I think I started to fall in love with you the first time I saw you behind the counter in the mercantile. The day we had our picnic, I knew then you were the only man I'd ever love. That's why I couldn't marry Curly. If I couldn't have you, I didn't want anyone else."

He wrapped his arms around her and kissed her.

"Now it's my turn to play 'what if'," she said through her tears once he released her. "I asked you to marry me the first time we met. What if I asked you again now?"

"I'd say yes. Absolutely yes."

"Then I think we'd better go find ourselves a preacher."

EPILOGUE

Sybil stood on the porch of the ranch house and rested her hands on the railing as she looked out over the meadows. The view never failed to soothe her, especially at this time of day when the sky was streaked with scarlet and orange and gold and the sun dipped behind the mountains in the distance.

Beside her, six-month-old Molly lay in her cradle, making baby noises and chewing on her tiny fist.

The door opened behind her and Devin came up behind her. He wrapped his arms around her waist and drew her back into him, moving her hair and planting a quick kiss on her neck. She covered his hands with hers and rested her head on his chest, contentment flowing through her.

"Do you know what day it is?" she asked him.

His expression grew serious. "Did I miss something important?"

"Very important," she replied. "Today is the third anniversary of my father's death."

He didn't speak for a moment, then nodded. "It is, isn't it? I'm sorry I forgot."

"You've been busy."

"So the Franklin Ranch is finally yours," he said softly.

She shifted in his arms, turning her head to look up at him. "Ours," she contradicted. "The ranch is ours. Yours and mine. No longer the Franklin Ranch, but the Franklin-McGregor Ranch. And we both know you're the one who's responsible for what we've accomplished so far."

There was still a lot of work to be done, and it would take years to reach the level of success her father had achieved. It had taken months of back-breaking labor before the fences were repaired and the grazing land was ready so they could get their cattle back from Joel Hutchings.

They'd added to the herd, and the cattle were healthy and well-fed, and the calves born that spring were thriving.

"Things have worked out pretty well, haven't they?" he asked.

"More than well," she said, looking out at the corrals and the grazing land beyond. Her gaze drifted to the sky.

Although sadness always overshadowed this day

every year, and she still wished she could have known the man who'd made this possible, she smiled, sure in her heart that he was watching from above.

And he was pleased.

ABOUT THE AUTHOR

Margery Scott is the author of more than twenty-five novels, novellas and short stories in various genres. Although she grew up as far away from the old west as possible, Margery has always admired the men and women who settled the untamed land west of the Mississippi. Glued to TV westerns like Maverick, Rawhide and Gunsmoke, and reading stories of Annie Oakley, Roy Rogers and Rin Tin Tin, it was only natural that when she started writing, she wrote what she loved to watch and read. She now lives on a lake in Canada with her husband, and when she's not writing or travelling in search of the perfect setting for her next novel, you can usually find her wielding a pair of knitting needles or a pool cue.

Website: www.margeryscott.com
Email: margery@margeryscott.com

Follow Margery on:
Facebook: www.facebook.com/AuthorMargeryScott
Twitter: www.twitter.com/margeryscott
Bookbub: www.bookbub.com/authors/margery-scott
Instagram: www.instagram.com/margeryscott48

www.ingramcontent.com/pod-product-compliance
Lightning Source LLC
Chambersburg PA
CBHW030816200726
48288CB00004B/1255